I0743161

# The DEATHS of ADAM JONES

## (SPACE JUNK BOOK 3)

## ANDREW BIXLER

PIP

Published by Pants Team Press.



For more information about this book and to receive updates on new releases, visit **andrewbixler.com**

Cover illustration by Chun Lo
Interior illustrations by Gary Bixler

ISBN: 978-1-7370607-3-4

**Books by Andrew Bixler**

Space Junk: Beginning no End

Space Junk

More Space Junk

The Deaths of Adam Jones
(Space Junk Book 3)

Pants Team Pink: Shameless Promotional Adventure
(Space Junk Book 4)

This one's for all the lost souls


Special thanks once again to Meghan Lear for cleaning this thing up and Gary Bixler for providing the interior illustrations.

# PART 1

Life

# 1-5

In the beginning, there was light – the blinding fluorescent kind. And it all went downhill from there.

As my aching eyes adjust to their new reality, the frigid air stinging my naked skin, I'm met by a roomful of towering, waxen monsters. A sense of excitement stirs amongst the throng of gruesome spectators as I'm carried across the featureless chamber toward a moaning, red-faced creature splayed out on a blood and sweat stained birthing apparatus. As the creature extends its gangly appendages, I squirm in my captor's arms, and my slimy, ill-formed body slips from its terrible grasp. The passage of time seems to slow then, and as the blood-spattered tile hurtles toward me, the very first spark of a thought begins to form in the back of my undeveloped brain. Vague and unintelligible, it's something to the effect of *'oh chit!'*

*"That's it?"* the young soul mentally moans, its green Stockwellian hair sticking out at all angles. The aura surrounding it is still clear and bright, undamped by the ill-effects of life in the universe. "Just like that, you're dead?"

After all this time, Adam's glow has been reduced to little more than a dingy gray haze clinging to his ethereal husk. "Not much to it, I know."

"But it wasn't even your fault!" the kid complains, struggling to comprehend. "That's not *fair.*"

*"Ha,"* Adam blurts, striking his bony knee. "If I had a murray for every death that wasn't my fault, I'd still be alive. Coming into the universe, like much of the rest of life, is a struggle. Anyway, that chidiot dropped me four more times before he got it right."

The kid's face droops. "You mean you died five times before you even escaped the delivery cubicle?"

"That's right," Adam says, with a tired nod. "Remembering it now is almost harder than living through it. Luckily, I was born with plenty of murrays. Plus, I found out the doctor died a couple times slipping on the afterbirth, so there's that…"

"Sounds like a nightmare," the kid thinks.

"Oh, it is. But only most of the time." Groaning under the weariness wrought by more lifetimes than he can remember, Adam pushes himself up from the worn chair and motions for the young spirit to follow him out of the cluttered den. "Come on, all this reminiscing is making me thirsty."

"I'll never get used to these fraiching legs," the soul complains, clambering to her feet. "How come you don't float around like everyone else?"

Adam shrugs as he shuffles down the hall, the old salvaged floorboards creaking underneath him. "It reminds me of life in the universe."

"Well, then how come I have to use them?"

Stepping into the dim kitchen, he yanks open the fridge door and says, "My house, my rules."

The kid soon follows, stumbling through the warped doorway. Her chosen appearance is almost human, with long, gangly limbs and big eyes. But there's something uncanny about it, like her designer got everything just a little bit wrong.

"Aren't murrays allocated based on ability?" she thinks out loud. "In other words, the more murrays a soul gets, the lower its competence?"

"Well…," Adam says, considering it as he cracks a cold one. "I don't think that's true."

"I don't get any of this!" she whines, her face twisting into a pitiful grimace as her agitation grows, and suddenly the questions start spilling out. "How come you live in this weird house? And why do you keep drinks in that box? Why do you drink anything at all? How come you look so old? What's with all the junk piled up around here? Is the whole universe this confusing? *Why the fraiche are you looking at me like that?*"

Adam laughs and pats the young soul on the shoulder. "You remind me of a younger, dumber me."

"*Awww,*" the kid cries.

"Don't worry so much," he says, reaching into the fridge. "Here, have a beer."

"I can manifest my own drink," she thinks.

"You can't manifest this." Adam cracks the can and sets it on the table. "It was only available in the universe for a very short period during a timeline that was retconned out of existence. Very few souls had the pleasure of imbibing it during that brief brewing window. I just happened to be among the inebriated."

The kid's misshapen eyes grow wide as she reverentially lifts the can of Nü Guard to her mouth, sips the frothy contents, and spits it all over Adam's reproduction kitchen.

*"Ulchh,"* she thinks, manifesting a glass of water to wash the crisp, hoppy taste out of her mouth. "That's the worst thing I've ever had, and I've tried candy corn."

"It's an acquired taste," Adam admits. "Anyway, what do you know? Who the fish are you, again? I don't even know your name."

"I already told you, my name is *Cromula.*"

"Oh yeah…," he says. "Of course it is. Well, what are you doing here? I was right in the middle of a really good movie."

"I told you that too," Cromula thinks, throwing her ethereal hands up in exasperation. "I've been studying to prepare for my first life in the universe, and I came to learn firsthand about what it's like."

"But why'd you come to me? There's no shortage of souls who lived in the universe."

"Because…" Wincing, Cromula hauls herself up onto her wobbly legs and stands at attention. "From everything I've learned, you're the greatest space pirate who ever lived."

"Well, obviously that's true," Adam says. "But what could I possibly teach you?"

"We've been studying your deaths," she explains. "But I can tell there's more to them than what's available in the

Asskashik records. I want to learn about them from the source. I think they may be the secret to a better life."

"I promise you," Adam says, sighing, "the only secrets my deaths hold are the incidental bumblings of an old space pirate. Plus, it would take too long to watch them all. There's sort of a lot of them…"

"You don't understand," the kid thinks. "I've learned everything I can from the official accounts. The only way to prepare for this kind of thing is to face it head on. I promise, I'll be the best student you ever had. *Ple-ease*…"

"It is a shame to let them go unwatched." Rubbing his sagging chin as he looks into the spirit's pitiful ill-proportioned features, and despite his better judgment, he finally decides, "What the space hell."

Waving for her to follow, Adam leads the kid out of the kitchen and down the main corridor of the ancient ghost house. Everything looks exactly the way it did the last time he was inside the real thing. Or maybe it doesn't. Just as his memories have warped and faded over time, so too, he figures, has his imaginary home. Sometimes he finds what he thinks are little, almost imperceptible changes in the pattern of a rug or the face in a picture. But he can never be sure. The only thing he *is* sure of is that nothing stays the same.

As he climbs the warped staircase, he glances back at his visitor, stuck at the bottom as she tries to figure out how to scale the tall steps. Despite her obvious frustration with the foreign architecture, she regards everything in his house with the kind of awe normally reserved for those old souls who cured some terrible illness or invented a more efficient way of getting plastered.

"Hurry up, will yuh?" he calls down to her.

When she finally reaches the top, she thinks, "Whew! I think I'm starting to get the hang of these legs."

"Good," he tells her. "Now, prepare to be entertained."

The young soul glances over Adam's shoulder, and her eyes grow wide as she lays eyes on his video collection. Much larger than the true dimensions of the house could possibly accommodate, the room is crammed from wall to distant wall with shelves full of colorful rectangles surrounded by cardboard standees and all the novelty promotional items Adam could dredge up from the remotest corners of his mind. He even recreated the plastic paneling and stale popcorn scent of his favorite video rental store.

"Whoa, what is all this?" Cromula asks.

Waving his arm over the room with a dramatic flourish, Adam says, "These are the tapes of my life. All the defining moments are here, stored on thirty-four million or so VHS, for easy access."

"*Wow…*," Cromula thinks. "That's the weirdest thing I've ever heard. Like, why don't you keep them on something smaller, or just access them in your mind?"

"Because I can't trust my memory," Adam explains. "Storing them like this, I know they won't ever change. At least, I don't think they will… Anyway, you should be praising my exceptional foresight for creating and thus providing you access to such a collection. So, have at it."

As the old space pirate limps back toward the staircase, Cromula calls out, "Wait, where are you going? I don't know how to work these things. Plus, I need you to provide commentary."

"Are you kidding?" Adam grumbles.

"How else am I supposed to know what you were thinking?" she whines. "And how will I know how you felt before, after, and during each memory?"

Adam whispers ancient expletives under his breath as he grabs one of the tapes off the wall of deaths. "I can't believe this. Kid shows up on my doorstep and I'm just supposed to let her poke through my most painful, embarrassing memories." Shoving the tape into a specially-designed player mounted in the wall, the holo-lantern boots and his memory starts to play out around them. But before he can commence the narration, the doorbell chimes. *"Grahh,"* he groans, appealing to a force greater than himself. "Now who the fish is that?"

6.-7

"So, what do you think?" the one called Dad asks, wiping the sweat from his forehead before smacking the hull of their new old junker. "Needs a little work, but she made it back here in one piece."

"I don't know, Kren…" Mom's tired face scrunches as she glances down at me, gurgling in her arms. But the only support I can offer comes in the form of spit bubbles. "It looks sort of *really* dangerous. And what is that, a joke?" she asks, pointing at the words painted on the hull.

"That's the name my dad gave her – *Asteroid Jones.*" With his chest out and fists on hips, like some sort of super humanoid, Dad proudly admires the ship's clumsy construction. "The old man built this junker with his bare hands. Now it's ours, and it's gonna help us build a life. Before you know it, we'll be able to get off this rented rock and move to a nice planet somewhere, with tall trees and warm breezes."

Mom frowns at the ugly metal box, not much bigger than our crumbling moon shack, and tells him, "Well you're not getting me in that heap until the plumbing works." He steps closer to wipe the moon dust from her cheek, and her face softens. "But I like the sound of that."

Beaming, Dad takes me from her arms and tosses me into the air. I experience a few space seconds of panic, but his excitement is contagious, and suddenly I'm laughing as I fly out of his hands and up toward the stars. In that brief moment, all is right with the universe.

"And then the cheap dome we were renting got struck by a stray beer can." The doorbell rings again and Adam shouts, "I said I'm coming!"

"You mean you were all killed by a fluke piece of space junk?" Cromula asks, incredulous as the two of them fumble down the stairs. "This is beginning to sound like the worst universe ever."

"It's not always so dumb, but violent decompression is a fact of life." When they reach the bottom of the staircase, the bell rings again, and Adam stomps to the front of the house. "Whoever keeps ringing that bell is about to get a slipper up their sacred…" But when he yanks the door back, he's met by a familiar angelic face.

"Boy, you look old," the holy functionary says, its red hair wild and bright.

"Buttlicker," Adam grouses, chuckling bitterly. "At least the name never gets old."

"Actually, your relentless ridicule got me to thinking I should up with the times. So, I decided to change it. From now on, you can call me Buttmuncher…"

Adam stares at the angel for a long moment but ultimately decides not to press the issue. "So, what do you want? I hope you're not here to convince me to go back to life, because the answer is the same as last time — I'm retired."

"Didn't Crom tell you?" BM steps aside, and Adam notices a pack of young souls crowded in his front yard, clumsily chasing after his pets. "I thought you could teach them a thing or two about how to live in the universe, and how not to."

"*Ack!*" Adam cries and quickly grabs the door handle, but BM sticks a foot in the frame before he can pull it shut. "If you'd just move your foot, I could forget about all this."

Shoving the door back, BM says, "You've been cooped up in there with your videotapes for long enough. It's not healthy spending so much time in your own head. Anyway, I told these kids they'd get to learn from the greatest space pirate who ever sailed the black sea."

"Well, I won't argue with that…," Adam says.

"Great, then it's settled." Turning back toward his wispy wards, BM yells, "Hurry up and get inside, before he changes his mind."

Adam barely avoids being trampled as a quarter-dozen young souls race past him into the house, and he's powerless to stop them as they paw through his precious life baubles and old magazines.

"This is a fate worse than death," he laments.

"All right, enough messing around," BM tells them. "Do you want to kill him all over again? We're here to learn, not play with his stuff."

The pack of malformed miscreants quickly surrounds Adam to gawk at his shriveled form and assault him with mental chatter. Like Cromula, their features are exaggerated, as if designed by someone who has seen the universe but has never actually been there.

"This is Asteroid Jones?" a pixelated boy with a bright pink mohawk complains. "He looks more like Asteroid *Old*."

"Butt up, Ham," Cromula warns the kid. "Mr. Jones is doing us a favor."

"That's right," BM says. "But don't give him too much credit. He owes me. Big time."

"For what?" Adam demands.

"Uh, you know, all kinds of stuff," the angel says. "I've helped you out during your lives in ways you don't even know about."

Resigning himself to this annoying turn of events, Adam hunches over and whimpers, "Just tell me what you want so I can finish rewatching *The Stupids* in peace."

"It's my job to prepare these kids for life in the universe," BM explains. "As one of my most inexplicable triumphs, I've been teaching them all about your exploits. But there's still a lot of fear and uncertainty surrounding one topic. I figured, what better way to learn about death than from the expert?"

Adam tries to rouse himself to kick the trespassers out of his house, but he can't find the energy. "*Fine*. But we're not starting over. If you want to know about the deaths we've already covered, ask your green-haired friend here.

And if you want to learn from me, you have to follow my rules. Rule one, no touching my stuff. I don't want your disgusting fingers altering my reality. And two, no more projecting your thoughts. When you're with me, you gotta walk and you gotta talk."

"*Aww*, that's not fair," a small girl with rainbow hair and a face plastered in sparkling makeup psychically whines. "It's too hard."

"Sorry D'ohry," BM says. "But as long as Mr. Jones is your teacher you have to follow his rules."

"Now that that's settled," Adam grumbles, "let's get this over with."

He directs the kids to the staircase, and by the time he catches up to them, they're already bouncing between the display shelves mixing up his tapes.

"Rule number one," he shouts. *"Rule number one!"* Snatching a video from the pixely boy's hand, he announces, "Everyone put down the tapes and come sit on the tile."

The kids reluctantly follow his instructions, but they continue to squirm as he retrieves death number seven off the shelf and sticks it in the player.

"Before we start, I want to warn you that what you're about to see may be disturbing for some audiences." The girl with the green hair enthusiastically waves her hand, and Adam points at her. "You have a question, uh…"

"It's Cromula, remember? I was wondering why you need so many of these storage rectangles when all your memories could easily fit inside just one of them?"

Adam sighs, taking a moment to calm himself, and points to the boy sitting in back. "I have them for the same reason that kid wears sunglasses inside — for fun.

Plus, storing them this way makes browsing a lot easier. Now, are there any other questions?"

The boy with the neon sunglasses and one of those t-shirts that look like a tuxedo raises his hand. "Yeah, I got a question. What is wrong with you?"

"All right, that's enough questions," Adam says, turning off the lights as the memory is projected around them. "Ooh, this is a good one. It's the time when I accidentally opened the emergency escape hatch. We all lost a murray that space day…"

Sunglasses chimes in, "*Ha*, why the fraiche would you do that?"

"*Spuckler*," BM scolds, and the kids giggle.

"It's sort of hard to explain," Adam says. "It takes a few space years to get your bearings. It's like, when you're young you're stupid. Or at least stupid*er*…"

"I have a question," the sparkly girl calls out, her hand shooting up. "I'm D'ohry. Um, how is this supposed to help us?"

Shrugging, the old scrapper says, "I have no idea."

As the memory of inadvertently killing his entire family nears its graphic conclusion, Adam hears a bunch of tapes crash to the floor somewhere in the dark, and he whips his head around. Glaring at the circle of kids, he realizes that one of them is missing, and he mentally flicks on the lights to find a young spirit hovering around the wall of deaths.

Guiltily standing over the jumbled pile of video memories, the pixelated boy holds up one of the tapes and asks, "What happened to the last one?"

Adam storms across the room and snatches the case out of the kid's hand, but his anger immediately morphs into panic as he discovers that the tape of his final death is missing. The only thing inside case number '129' is a folded slip of paper with his name on it, which reads,

*Your tape is mine now, space pirate!*
<3 Daizy

8-9

"Adam, we've got a surprise for you!" Mom calls from a distant corner of the moon shack.

The sound of her voice overwhelms me. I can literally feel the excitement in the air. Having just about mastered getting around on my stomach, I take off wriggling across the playroom. Electric chatter fills the hallway as I pull myself along the dusty floor with the sense that something incredible is about to happen.

"I guess he doesn't want to see it," Dad teases.

My limbs are starting to get tired, but nothing can stop me now. Whatever I'm missing out on is just around the corner. When I get within reach, I grab the door frame and with my last bit of strength, I drag myself through the opening and into the next room.

"What do you think?" Dad asks, smacking the bulky machine. "Can you believe somebody scrapped this old holo-tube? All it needed was a new heat sink."

When he flips the switch, the world suddenly comes alive with cartoon spaceships chasing each other around the furniture and exploding in magnificent multi-colored fireballs. All I know as I lift myself onto my knees, unblinking, is that I want that. I'm not sure how, but before I know what's happening, I'm on my feet.

"*Look*," Mom says. "I think he's going to walk. Would you take your eyes off that stupid gadget for one space second?" She crouches down to cheer me along, and I take a step forward.

"He's doing it," Dad says.

Somehow I manage to swing my leg around, and suddenly I'm lurching across the room. For a moment I think I'm going to fall, but I manage to keep my balance, and by my fifth step it feels like the universe will soon be bowing down to my incredible power.

"You're almost there," Mom says waving to me.

"Watch it," Dad warns. "He's coming right at you."

Arms outstretched, she prepares for impact, but at the last space second, I lunge past her to embrace my new best friend – the TV.

"I entered that room as Adam, but when I left, I was Asteroid Jones."

"Nuh uh," his green-haired trespasser says. "My research indicates that you didn't become Asteroid Jones until sometime during the Fan Wars."

"Well, this is when it really happened," Adam claims. "Who do you trust more, me or some eternal permanent record?"

"Uh…"

Spuckler raises his hand, evidently paying *some* attention behind his novelty sunglasses. "Hold up. You seemed fine. How did you die?"

"Apparently the intense joy I experienced overloaded my system. It's an unusual phenomenon. You see…" But as he begins to explain, he can feel their attention drifting back toward his videotapes. "That's not important. Let's move on to the next one. I think this is where I stick a fork in the electrical outlet."

"Yawn," D'ohry says, her sparkly pink lips forming a contemptuous smirk. "This is real interesting and everything. But I want to know why Daizy stole your memory. Was she mad at you or something?"

"How do you know about her?" Adam grumbles.

"Is your mind slipping?" Ham asks, his pixelated arm buried inside a bag of something that vaguely resembles popcorn. "We told you. The venerable Buttmuncher has been teaching us all about your life, for some reason."

"Hey, there's no eating in here," Adam snaps, snatching the bag out of the boy's greasy fist. "If you must know, I was mad at her. She wanted me to get rid of my tapes, and when I refused, she took off without a note or anything. Well, I guess she did leave a note…"

"In the one place she knew you'd find it," Cromula says.

"*Awww,*" the girls squeal.

"We should go find her!" D'ohry suggests.

"It's out of the question," Adam says. "If she wants to see me, she knows where I am."

But when his guardian angel hears them, it stops browsing and steps away from the display shelves of the old space pirate's vast memory collection to butt in. "I think it's a good idea."

"*What?!*" Adam cries. "Would you stay out of this? If I'm not here, all my stuff will fade."

"You won't be gone that long," BM says. "Anyway, it'll do you all good to get out of this attic and go on a real adventure."

"What about the rest of Mr. Jones's deaths?" Cromula pipes up, her green hair standing on end. "Unlike the rest of these lost souls, I actually want to learn something."

But the great know-it-all just scoffs. "Not to worry. Adam can take care of that. Right?"

"Well, technically," Adam admits. "But I'm not going to be happy about it."

"See?" BM says. "No problem."

Mumbling holy obscenities, Adam steps over to the wall of deaths and uses his near-limitless divine powers to shrink the tapes down small enough to fit into a small shoulder pack. "If we're going, then let's go. At least I'll get my tape back. All of a sudden, I can't remember what's on it."

At BM's urging, the kids all pile down the ancient staircase and out onto the porch, where Adam recites an ancient protection prayer, "Bless this mess."

The kids' expressions of awe and wonder as they gaze up at the artificial night sky surrounding Grandpa's old house reminds him of just how magical the universe used to seem.

As the class uses the hose to fill their canteens with holy water, a shrill voice suddenly cries out, "*Whoa, whoa, where do you think you're going?*"

"Aww, who is this?" Cromula asks, lifting the bright-eyed feline and petting its dark fur.

"That's just Ol' Garth," Adam says. "He's a space cat I found while I was out scrapping in an abandoned moon town."

Wriggling out of Crom's arms, the cat lands in the dead grass and stares up at Adam through wet eyes. "You're just going to leave me without any food?"

"You can feed yourself," Adam argues.

"But I like it better when you do it."

Glaring at the cat, Adam manifests a bowl of mashed meat and tosses it down. But as he leads the class through the cluttered yard, he turns to find Ol' Garth trailing them, his food bowl hovering close by.

"What do you want now?" he asks.

"Well, I can't very well stay here," the cat tells him. "Who will feed me?"

*"Gahh,"* Adam groans. "I thought the afterlife was supposed to be a relaxing place where you can do what you want without anyone bothering you."

*"Pff,"* BM scoffs. "What the fraiche gave you that idea?"

When they reach the end of the yard, the kids rush to look out over the edge into the bottomless void below. Lifting his sunglasses, Spuck manifests a rock and tosses it in the pit just to watch it disappear.

"So, what do we do now, just warp over to the other side?" Crom asks.

"Chit no," Adam says. "I'm way too old for that kind of travel. Rule number two – when you're with me, you gotta walk."

He points behind them to a long, crumbling rope bridge tethering his little reality to the rest of the space heavens, and their youthful faces suddenly put on a few hundred years.

"How the fraiche are we supposed to get across that?" D'ohry cries. "I've barely started to get a hang of these legs."

Approaching the bridge, Buttmuncher shakes one of the ropes. "Seems sturdy enough. Incidentally, this feels like a good time to take my leave."

"What the fish are you talking about?" Adam growls. "You're the one who got us into this!"

"And it appears you have everything under control," the angel says. "You don't need me for this next part. Anyway, I've got other duties to attend."

"First of all, you said doody," Adam points out. "Second, you can't leave me in charge of these kids." Glancing out over the bottomless pit, he posits, "What if I lose one or don't feel like doing this anymore?" But when he turns back, the angel is already gone. "That sneaky fishing…"

"Hey, where'd our teacher go?" Ham asks, nervously rubbing his blocky arms as he glances around the yard.

"Your 'guardian angel' has abandoned you," Adam announces. "Let that be your first lesson – in the universe, the only one you can count on is yourself. However, seeing as you wouldn't stand a chance on your own, and since even the powers that be have apparently left you to fend for yourselves, it appears that I will have to guide you."

The kids glance at each other skeptically as Adam approaches the bridge and carefully steps out onto the first plank. Pleased with his progress, he turns back and beckons them to follow. One by one, they line up behind him and carefully make their way onto the shaky structure.

"Does this bridge look familiar to anyone?" Due to either soul-shaking fear or plain disinterest, no one answers, so Adam tells them, "It's a screen accurate replica of the one used in *The Temple of Doom*."

"What the fraiche is that?" Spuck asks, hanging onto his sunglasses.

"It's a movie," Adam says, "arguably the most horrific entry in the franchise."

"How are we supposed to know that?" the kid complains.

"I knew that!" Ham cries as he forces his flickering legs forward. "I know all the movies from your life. But isn't that the one where he cuts the rope?"

Just then, something on the bridge snaps, and it wavers under their feet.

"Hang on!" Adam yells, and falling to his stomach, he grabs onto the nearest plank.

The kids follow his lead, whimpering as they wrap their arms through the ropes. There's another loud snap, and they scream as the bridge swings down and smacks against the side of the dark cliff, sending a few planks and Ol' Garth tumbling into to the dark pit below.

"We have to climb," Adam says.

Scaling the decomposing rope ladder, he drags himself over the edge of the cliff and reaches back down to help the kids up. As soon as they're safe, they tearfully cling to the consecrated ground, and he impatiently waits for them to recover.

"I haven't done that in while," he says. "It was a little scarier than I remembered." As his 'students' gradually get back on their feet, he taps the support beam at the end of the bridge, and it falls in reverse, swinging back up into its original position and reattaching itself to the other side of the pit.

"You mean it fell on purpose?" Cromula moans.

"Of course," Adam says. "If you watched the movie, you would have known that was going to happen. Call it lesson number two."

"But you almost killed us!" Sparkly tears stream down D'ohry's cheeks as the young souls console each other. "And what about Ol' Garth? You just let him fall."

The fabric of reality near the bridge starts to appear all wiggly, and Ol' Garth suddenly materializes by the edge of the cliff. The cat indifferently glances at the gawking kids and then proceeds to clean itself.

"So, none of that was real?" Crom whines.

Adam shrugs.

"Then why did you make us do it?" she asks.

"How many times do I have to say it?" he grouses. "For fun!"

# 10

"He can't see!" Mom cries as I crane my neck toward the window. "Are you sure this is a good idea? Isn't he a little young to be flying the ship?"

*"Too young?"* the knobby humanoid they call Grandpa says, leaning over me to stick a picture of the two of us up on the window before plunking down in the kiddie seat. "I taught Kren to fly this very ship before he could walk!"

"I had to learn that part on my own…" Stuffed next to Mom in the passenger seat, Dad reaches across the aisle and yanks on a bar under my chair, raising it so that I can see over the edge of the dash. "But Adam is gonna be fine." He moves my hand to a big lever on the control board and tells me, "I already set the autopilot. All you have to do is take her home…"

"I can't watch," Mom says, her hands over her eyes.

I do as Dad instructs, pushing on the lever, and the ship begins to accelerate.

"Look at that," Grandpa says. "He's a natural, or my name isn't Silas Ichabod Jones."

Emboldened by my success, I shove the accelerator forward, and my body is thrown back against the seat, my fingers raking over the dash as the ship takes off toward the not-so-distant rock called home.

"We're going too fast," Mom wails.

I try to lift my arm to slow us down, but the force pressing on me is too great. "I can't move!"

"Don't worry," Dad tells us as he wrenches himself up from his seat. "I have the speed control set." But when he tries to pull the lever back, it won't budge.

Her fingers digging into the armrest, Mom cries, "Why aren't we slowing down?"

"He must have locked the controls somehow," Dad says, frantically prodding the dashboard.

"How the fish did he do that? I didn't even know that was a thing." The veins in her arms and face swelling, Mom somehow manages to push herself up from her seat, and grabbing onto the collar of Dad's spacesuit, she screams, *I told you this was a bad idea!*

"From out there, our crummy little moon shack didn't look so bad," Adam muses. "I mean, until we were crashing into it."

"That's an interesting death," Crom says, the collapsing bridge outside Adam's house all but forgotten as she jots something in her sticker-plastered notebook. "I sense there is much to learn from it."

"Yeah," Adam says, stuffing the portable memory player back in his bag. "The lesson is, don't let the kids fly the ship."

As the rest of the class recovers from their fake brush with death to gaze out at the vast stretch of bright countryside surrounding them, D'ohry runs her fingers through her rainbow hair and asks, "So, how do we find Daizy?"

"Luckily, she left a forwarding address," Adam says, digging in his pocket for the note she left. "You know, in case anyone came looking for her."

"Like you?" the girl asks.

"I don't know what you mean," Adam tells her as he squints at the paper. "But it says she moved to the other side of Other Side. The only way to get there is by going through the Forest of Lost Souls. If you look close, you can see it from here. It's always out there, near the edge of creation."

Adam points his boney finger, and the kids turn their attention to a formless mass of dark trees in the distance.

"I've heard of that place," Ham tells them, flickering. "They say once you go in, you never come out."

"Sounds like a load to me," Adam says.

"Can we *please* just warp through?" Spuck begs, his sunglasses slipping down his nose as he gazes out at their distant destination.

Trying not to lose his patience, Adam reminds him, "Rule two! Walking is part of living in the universe. Plus, instantaneous travel makes me sick. Anyway, it's too dangerous. The forest has a way of confusing tourists. We don't want to get trapped between planes."

"Then can't we just, like, go around?" the boy asks. "This place doesn't sound very sandal-friendly."

"The forest is infinitely wide," Adam says. "So no. The only way around is through. You'll all be fine. You're blank slates. You've got nothing for it to throw at you. I'm the one who really needs to be careful."

"Well, I'm in," Crom announces, and mentally tying her green hair back, she transforms her outfit from disheveled student to pseudo-Space Scout. "If this is what it takes to live a good life, then let's do it."

Groaning, the rest of them trudge after her into the greater unknown, when Adam shouts, "Wait a space second! We gotta go next door first and ask The Colonel to watch my pets and all my stuff while I'm gone."

"Do you really think that's necessary?" Crom asks, her hands on her hips. "Who's going to steal from you?"

"You never know…"

Wandering over to the plot next door, Adam leads the kids through the open fence and down a dirt path roaming with bizarre poultry and other altogether unidentifiable manifestations. The objects, like the muddled imaginings of a spacehead made real, have no precedence in the universe and so are impossible to describe. Fortunately, none of Adam's wards ask him to try.

The house is surrounded by an overgrown scrapyard littered with discarded promotional materials and half-baked gastronomic creations. Some of them are physical in form while others exist merely as nebulous thoughts floating through the ether. Adam suddenly feels inspired to create some sort of dancing fish waffle, but he shakes off the idea as he approaches the decaying bungalow and knocks on the screen door.

"Come on in," a high-pitched, jowly voice calls from somewhere inside.

Adam cautiously leads the kids into the ancient house, stepping over piles of greasy fast food wrappers and the moldy leftovers from countless failed culinary experiments. When they reach the kitchen, they find The Colonel slaving over a bubbling grease vat.

The sleeves of his white suit rolled up, the old prophet uses his tongs to fish a hunk of fried meat out of the scalding oil and tosses it to Adam. "Try that."

"*Ah, ooh,*" Adam yelps, juggling the sizzling thigh between his hands until it's cool enough to handle. Unable to identify the strange meat, he takes a sizeable bite and immediately spits it back out.

"Well, how is it?" The Colonel asks, his white hair matted with sweat.

"It's really… *awful,*" Adam says. "What is it?"

"Dang it!" Wiping his hands, the old chef snaps his towel over his shoulder and shakes his head. "It's cultured Morlock. I thought cooking it the old-fashioned way might fix the flavor."

"Well that's…," Adam says. "Anyway, I came to ask if you'd do me a favor and keep an eye on my place while I usher these kids through the Forest of Lost Souls? I don't think it'll take very long."

"A course," The Colonel says, smacking Adam on the back. "What are neighbors for?"

When the old man isn't looking, Spuck and Ham sneak a couple pieces of fried Morlock and loudly gag on the rancid meat.

"This stuff tastes like how I imagine death feels," Spuck cries, wiping his greasy fingers on his tuxedo t-shirt. "Who is this old codger, anyway?"

"*Codger?*" The Colonel bristles. "I'll have you know I brought peace to the universe – *twice*. First I gave them the Ten Commandments, which were *very* popular. Then I followed that up with my famous Eleven Herbs and Spices."

"Speaking of…" As Adam glances around the sty, he can't help but think maybe The Colonel's talents are being squandered. "Have you ever thought about going back to life?"

"It's all I think about," the old man says. "But do you know how many lives it took me to get a second hit? This time I'm goin' back prepared. I'm just havin' a little trouble comin' up with twelve of something."

Mumbling through a mouthful of pre-chewed Morlock meat he scavenged off the floor, Ol' Garth says, "Well, I for one think you've found another winner."

"Excuse me, Mr. Colonel," Crom interjects. "But you're such an old soul, is there anything you can teach us about how to do life?"

The Colonel's brow creases and he rubs his white beard as he thinks it over. Finally raising his finger, he says, "The important thing to remember when it comes to life is… that is to say, the secret to living in the universe is… what I mean is, yuh jist gotta let yer freak flag fry."

"Well, this has been very informative," Adam says. "But we'd better be off. The sooner we leave, the sooner I can get back and finish my movie."

"I know!" The Colonel announces. "The key to life is to always be… that is, you gotta keep your head… I'm sure I wrote it down here somewhere."

As the old man furiously searches his recipe books for the meaning of life, Adam quietly guides the kids out of the kitchen and back down the cluttered hallway.

"What the fraiche is that guy's problem?" Ham asks, his blocky body blurring as they find their way out.

"*Shhh*," Adam says. "He's okay. He's just been here for a *really* long time."

"*I've got it!*" The Colonel shouts from behind them as they scamper across the lawn. Pushing through the screen door, he yells after them, "*The secret of life is to always keep your fryer on. Hold on, at least take a bucket of Morlock!*"

# 11–12

"Why can't I just stay home and watch TV with you guys?"

"Because," Mom says as she guides the *Asteroid Jones* through the atmosphere of a small moon orbiting the local dump planet.

When it becomes clear that she's done explaining, I ask, "Because why?"

"Because I said so, that's why," she tells me, resorting to the old standby. "You can't spend all your time cooped up inside that crummy moon shack. You have to learn… stuff and make friends with people your own age. And I don't know what you think we do all day, but your father and I will be out scrapping together a living, not watching TV."

"*We get it,*" a croaking voice announces in back. "*Or he gets it, or you get it,* you get it?"

"I can hear him watching right now!" I complain.

"Not for long," Mom assures me, pulling the ship down outside the gray rectangle where I'll be confined for the next ten space hours of my miserable life. "Now hurry up, or you're going to be late."

Stuffing a bag ration into my hands, she gives me a hug and shoves me through the airlock out to the space monsters. The crumbling grounds are overflowing with kids from all over the Rental Belt and beyond. Watching them howl and hang from the railings, I decide I'll take my chances with Mom, but when I turn back, she's already pulling away.

Clumsily fishing inside my pocket, I find and uncrumple my schedule, but deciphering the abbreviated class names and alien room numbers is hopeless. I try to keep my whimpering to a minimum as I scurry through the crowd toward the big flexiglass doors, but before I can reach them, someone snatches the paper from my hand.

"Need some help?" a gravelly voice asks, and I look back to find a towering space kid with black eyes and a sharp, crooked jaw staring down at me. "Don't worry, I'll show you exactly where to go."

"Y-you will?" I ask.

"Sure," the kid says, grinning. "And all it'll cost you is your rations."

"Oh…" Holding my lunch tight, I reach for the schedule in his hand. "That's okay. I can find it."

But as I lunge for the wrinkled paper, the kid holds it behind his back and snatches my lunch bag. "Gimme that."

The other kids are watching now, some laughing, and I can feel the tears welling as the bag slips through my fingers.

"This is *my* lunch," the kid says. "Maybe I could be convinced to share. But what are you gonna do for *me*?"

"I don't know," I whimper, realizing I'm about to start sobbing in front of the whole space school before I even get inside the building.

A cruel smile forms on the kid's face. "I know. How about you start by getting down on your knees and—"

"How about this?" someone says, and the kid's body suddenly convulses and goes limp, crumpling to the pavement.

My mouth drops, and for a moment all I can do is stare down at his twitching body.

"Don't worry," the voice says. "He'll be fine in a few space minutes. My mom gave me this thing for protection in case the school gets taken over by space gangs again. I didn't think I'd need to use it on the first day."

When I come to, I realize there's a small kid with mossy hair and coarse, green skin standing next to me. He hands me his fun taser and helps me collect my stuff. Having lost interest, the rest of the kids disperse, and my new friend urges me inside the building before my bully can recover.

Glancing at my schedule, the boy says, "Your class is down the hall on the left."

"Thanks a lot," I mutter, still coming to grips with what just happened. "Hey, what's your name?"

"I'm Brinx, Brinx Bartly."

"I'm Adam Jones." As the bell rings, I tell Brinx, "I don't know how I'm gonna make it for... how long do we have to do this?"

Taking off down the hall, Brinx yells, "Only, like, twelve more space years."

"That drained the life right out of me," Adam tells his disciples as they tramp through the green pastures of Other Side. "It might not sound like a long time to you, but it's twice as long as I had been alive at that point. Even now, the prospect of going back to school chills me to the depths of my eternal soul."

"So, like, what's the point?" Spuck asks, his hands stuffed in the pockets of his counterfeit board shorts.

"Point?" Adam cries. "There is no point. It's just what happened."

"But it doesn't make any sense," the boy says. "That kid was *huge*."

"Of course it makes sense!" Adam looks around at the others to confirm that they're following along, but even Cromula seems confused. "You have to remember that you're seeing things the way I experienced them, not necessarily as they actually happened." The once-bright glows emanating from his students have already faded considerably, and though still much more vibrant than his own, he has to remind himself that they're just kids. "Why don't we stop here and rest for a while?"

Gathering under the shade of a large, shimmering tree growing up out of the bright landscape, Adam replays the time he got trapped inside the ball crater at the local Moon Zone, and the mood starts to lift. For a brief moment, he even finds himself enjoying the kids' company.

As they discuss possible ways to avoid such tragedies,

Crom says, "There's some stuff I still don't get. Like, how come you can understand what everyone is saying when they're all speaking different languages? And what's that yellow ring floating over your head? It makes you look like a dork."

"Understanding all the languages in the universe is simple enough," Adam explains. "All it requires is a universal translator called a Babel chip. Back when I was alive, most people had them implanted at birth. The only problem was all the ads constantly being transmitted into your temporal lobe. But most of those could be eliminated by installing an ordinary ad blocker. As for the halo, I wear it to indicate that I'm dead."

"Of course you're dead," D'ohry points out, with a glittery smirk. "*You're here!*"

"Oh yeah…" Once the class has regained their energy, he pushes his old body up off the grass and leans against the sacred tree to peer out ahead. "Well, we better get moving. We've still got a long way to go."

As they prepare to resume their journey through the afterlife, Adam suddenly gets the feeling that he might never return. He glances back to take one final look at the old house, but his little bubble of space has already faded out of view.

Before long, the clear sky turns overcast, and a cold wind begins to blow. Adam has a hard time remembering the last time he experienced even moderate discomfort. As he rubs his arms for warmth, he considers canceling the trip altogether, but seeing the kids' determination toughing it out on their new legs, he forces himself to trudge on.

As they approach the edge of the heavenly realm, the terrain grows increasingly hostile. Lush, sweeping fields give way to rough, lifeless tracts of rocky soil. Their pace slows, and the ether surrounding them grows hazy, until they find themselves blindly tripping through a dense cloud of fog.

"Is everyone still here?" Adam calls out.

"I think so," Crom says. "D'ohry is with me, but we can't see where we're going."

Something suddenly crashes into Adam's back, and he finds Spuck feeling his way through the fog in his sunglasses.

"Oh spit," Ham yelps, followed by a loud splash.

"Ham?" Adam says, stumbling toward a faint light in the distance. "Where are you?"

"I'm okay," Ham finally answers. "Just a little wet."

As they make their way toward the boy's voice, the fog begins to lift, and the five of them, plus Adam's cat, find themselves standing on the edge of a murky lake.

"I'm fine too," Ol' Garth says, padding along the shore. "Not that anyone is paying attention."

Ignoring the needy cat, Adam says, "I forgot about the Moat of Despair… We'll have to cross it to get to the forest."

"How the fraiche are we supposed to do that?" Ham asks as he plods out of the water like a no-budget movie monster.

"I could swear there was a boat or something," Adam says, searching for the light he spotted in the fog. "*There…*"

A short ways down the shore, they come to a rotted dock reaching out into the dark water, its far end almost completely obscured by shadow and fog, with the exception of a distant orb of yellow light floating in the gloom.

Prodding the nearest plank with her flashing sneaker, D'ohry asks, "Is this going to be the same as the last bridge we crossed? Because I don't want to get wet."

"Of course not," Adam scoffs. "At least, I don't think so."

Despite his dubious assurances, the kids cautiously follow him across the precarious structure, and before long they've made it all the way to the other end without incident.

"Told you," the old space pirate says.

"*What do you want?*" a cold, piercing voice suddenly growls, nearly startling Adam to life, and a gaunt statue of a humanoid wrapped in tattered black rags steps out of the shadows.

"Uh, we request passage," Adam intones. "So, how does this work? What's the price?"

"The price…" The figure's decaying lips curl back, and it releases a horrifying cackle. "The price is your soul!"

The kids gasp, and for a space second Adam fears one of them is going to fall into the lake trying to escape.

"Really?" he asks the creature. "Because I visited a long time ago and I don't remember giving up my soul."

"It's a joke, for the kids," the ferryman says. "Just get in the boat."

# 13.-14

"This ship goes to the Rental Belt only," the bus driver warns her raucous passengers, scanning over them with piercing yellow eyes rumored to be capable of seeing into a kid's soul. A beefy eastern universal woman with a purple complexion and a single, perpetually furrowed eyebrow, Mrs. Krenk plops down behind the controls and whips her head around. "If any of you wind up on the wrong ship again, you're gonna spend the night at school."

"We sure as chit wouldn't want that, Mrs. *Crank*," the kid who tried to steal my lunch hollers, high-fiving one of his chidiot friends.

"Bimmy Jinx, is it?" The ship quiets as Mrs. Krenk rises from her seat and locks eyes with the bully. "If I have to get up from this chair again, you're all going to have a Merry Poncemas."

"What does that mean?" Bimmy asks.

"It means sit down and chut up!"

"That's what he gets," I whisper to Brinx in the next seat, and Krenk turns her yellow glare on me.

Before I know what I'm going to think, she says, "Don't even think about it."

She stomps back to her seat, and the chatter resumes as the ship takes off from the school parking lot. Once we're moving, Brinx and I take out our binders of Chibi Sitcom cards to see if we can work out a trade.

"There was only one pack left at the Moon Mart," Brinx complains. "But I got a card I need for my deck – Tiny Danza."

"Nice one," I tell him. "I haven't been able to find any more. The guy who runs the scrap shop keeps buying 'em all before they even make it to the shelf."

"What an ackle," Brinx says, looking over my cards. "His name's Krad. I hate that guy. Hey, what do you want for Knee-high Newhart?"

"That's one of the strongest cards in the game!" I cry, momentarily taken aback by his brazenness. "But I do only need one more Darryl to create the Six-eyed Slow-witted Woodsman…"

"Other Brother Darryl is yours," Brinx says, carefully slipping the card from its sleeve.

We seal the exchange of our cardboard treasures through the ancient covenant of the scrapper's handshake, when Other Brother Darryl is suddenly swiped from my fingers. Leaning over the back of the seat in front of us, Bimmy studies the card like he's never seen one before.

"What are these stupid things?" he asks.

"Uh, nothin'," Brinx says, playing it cool. "It's just a dumb card game."

"Oh yeah?" Bimmy looks me in the eye, as if sensing my fear, and says, "Then you won't care if I do this."

"*No!*" we both shout as he crumples the card and drops it at our feet.

"Don't make me stop this ship!" Mrs. Krenk shouts.

As we look down upon the senseless carnage, the bully skitters toward the front of the bus, cackling, "*Ah-hahaha.*"

In that moment, the silent strength of Other Brother Darryl lights a fire inside me, and before I can stop myself, I pick up the ball of cardboard and fling it at Bimmy's crooked jaw. But before it makes contact with its intended target, he ducks, and the crumpled card taps the back of Mrs. Krenk's wide head.

The ship slams to a stop, and the bus driver slowly rises from her seat. The fire in her eyes as she stomps toward me is like something out of a disciplinarian nightmare, but the scariest thing is the twisted smile stretched over her face.

Lost in torturous thought, Adam gazes out into the dense mist blanketing the moat. Hypnotic ashen wisps whirl across the dark water in thick, ghostly clouds, concealing the imaginary monsters that prowl its black depths. Leaning over the edge of the wooden boat, his distorted reflection stares back at him. He barely recognizes himself beneath the wrinkles and thin mat of silver hair. The vessel's wake warps his features into something grotesque, and he suddenly realizes that he's not looking at himself but at a decaying Mrs. Krenk, grinning at him from below the water's surface. He instinctively sticks his hand out to splash her away, when she reaches out and wraps her cold dead fingers around his wrist. Shrieking, he wrenches his arm back, but she just squeezes tighter.

"What is your problem?" Spuck asks.

Adam turns to beg for his students' help, but when he looks back, the monster is gone. They stare at him as he hyperventilates, glancing between them and the moat, until he calms down.

Sucking on the straw of a large soda, his pink mohawk flickering, Ham asks, "So, what the fish happened with the bus?"

"Oh, right," Adam says between big gulps of ether. "A few space seconds later, we were sideswiped by a multi-milk delivery ship. Of course, that was before emergency brakes were mandatory."

"This place gives me the creeps," D'ohry moans, huddled beside Crom in the back of the boat, her rainbow hair glowing in the dark.

"Don't worry, I think we're almost there." Adam looks to the ferryman for confirmation, but their skeletal captain just shrugs.

Squinting out into the fog, the old space pirate suddenly notices a dim pair of lights up ahead, and he figures they must have reached the far shore. But after a moment, he realizes that the hazy orbs are coming toward the boat, *fast*.

"Duck!" he screams, and the whole class gets down as the biggest delivery ship he's ever laid eyes on barrels at them through the mist. Curling into the fetal position, he squeezes his eyes tight and waits for the collision. But it never comes. After a little while, he lifts his head and glances around the boat to check on his students. "Did you see that?"

The kids skeptically glance at one another as they pick themselves up, and Crom asks, "See what?"

"Nothing," Adam tells them, climbing up onto the bench. "I was just testing you. You passed."

"Oh," she says. "Well… good."

As the fog rolls over them, Adam tries to keep his mind focused on happy thoughts, but he can feel the moat probing him for a way in.

"So, is this all you do?" Spuck asks the ferryman.

Turning his dead eyes on the dumb kid, the creature groans. "What do you mean? What else would I do?"

"Fraiche, I don't know," the kid says, lying back across the bench. "Like, literally anything."

"I guess I never thought about it before." The ferryman stops rowing for a long moment but finally returns to his eternal duty.

Despite his best effort, Adam can feel his thoughts wandering, and he begins absentmindedly fiddling with his tapes. Somehow, through a long and winding trail of memories, he ends up thinking of the time Dad 'taught' him how to swim, and he suddenly finds himself flailing in the deep end, gasping for air. He gets a lungful of black water and floats down into the dark for what seems like an eternity, until he feels someone grab onto his arms and drag him back up.

"Pull, you guys!" a familiar voice yells, and Adam flops back into the boat.

Wet and shivering, he warns the dark souls leaning over him, "Get away from me! You're not going to trick me again. Your disguises are very good. You almost had me convinced. But I'm onto you!"

"How the fraiche did he get out of the boat?" one of the demons asks, a row of sharp pink horns lining its skull. "I didn't even see it happen."

The one with green fire shooting out of the back of its head leans down for a closer look, and Adam cowers under the seat. "I think he's hallucinating."

"He said we wouldn't be affected, remember?" a small multi-colored monster tells the others. "We don't have as much spiritual baggage."

"So, what are we supposed to do now?" the bug-eyed party animal asks. "We have to snap him out of it."

"Stay back," Adam warns them. "I know what you're trying to do, and it won't work!"

As he holds them off, a slinky shadow creature slips out from underneath one of the seats, and as it glides across the boat, it tells the others, "I thought you knew everything there is to know about 'the greatest space pirate whoever whatevered.' I guess it's up to Ol' Garth to save the day, again." Hopping onto the bench across from Adam, the creature manifests a shiny cylinder and floats it across the boat. "There yuh go."

Transfixed by its mysterious beauty, Adam plucks the golden object out of the air. By instinct, he cracks the can, and as he consumes the ice cold contents, the dark souls surrounding him gradually transform back into his students.

Once he's regained his senses, he scratches Ol' Garth's head and tells his loyal pet, "Thank you, old friend. I owe you my eternal soul."

"Ahem…" The cat motions toward its empty bowl, and Adam fills it with the best ration pâté he ever ate. "Now we're even."

# 15

Judging by the stunned expression on Ms. Takajohnson's face, one of such utter disbelief that it seems like she might suddenly cease to exist, I don't think she knows what hit her. Seated around the table in front of our half-eaten lunches, the only thing the rest of us can do is stare in horror at the blob of gray ration goop dripping down the side of our teacher's face. Not even the perpetrator of the heinous act is bold enough to add insult to injury by laughing. For a moment, as she picks the sludge from her cropped yellow hair, she looks like she's going to cry. But then her soft features harden, and she turns toward us, red-faced and shaking with rage.

"That's it!" she screams, the patient warmth with which she usually conducts the class having burned away entirely. "I've had it with you dam kids. If you want to act like little monsters, I'll treat you like—"

But before she can finish her sentence, something so vile, so offensive, so unthinkable happens that I can barely believe my good fortune. I didn't even see where the second glob of moldy meat paste came from. Whether it was Bimmy or some other troublemaker, it's too much for the rest of us to resist. The urge to join in on the mayhem is just too great.

The next thing I know, I'm circling the room with the rest of the kids in a ration-fueled frenzy as Ms. Takajohnson threatens us with increasingly imaginative punishments. Some of the students fingerpaint profanities on the wall while others toss their toys out the window just to watch them smash. Climbing onto the teacher's desk, Bimmy looks out over the havoc he has wrought and decrees that school is officially canceled.

I question his authority and methods, but I like his message. Intoxicated by the prospect of school's end, I grab a shiny object off the table, intent on committing one of the most egregious acts known to kid kind, when Ms. Takajohnson spots me.

"Don't you dare," she warns, shoving kids back into their chairs and slapping away plastic projectiles as she moves toward me.

In a brief moment of sanity, I lower the scissors, but with the sounds of childhood revolution shouting in my ears, I think worse of it and take off running.

Shivering in his damp clothes, Adam throws his head back and sneezes, sending the portable memory player and what's left of his beer crashing to the bottom of the boat. "I don't have to tell you what happened next."

"*Yes you do*," Ham cries. "You can't just end on a cliffhanger like that."

Adam scoffs, his bony arms wrapped around his chest. "I impaled myself, of course." Concentrating on the warmest, most comfortable fabric he can dredge up from his life, he tries again to manifest a dry set of clothes. But it's no use. Although the living nightmares have ceased, his mind is still clouded.

"*Don't…* run… with… scissors," Crom says, writing in her travel notebook. "Makes sense."

"But what happened after that, at school?" D'ohry asks, the bright strands of her rainbow hair momentarily transforming into ravenous glow worms.

Ignoring the hallucination, Adam says, "Once the rush of rebellion wore off, things pretty much went back to normal."

"Back… to… normal," Crom says.

"You don't have to write that down," Adam tells her.

It feels like they've been drifting through the fog for eons when Spuck, lying across the back bench with his sunglasses propped on his forehead, moans, "*Are we there yet?*"

Adam had been so wrapped up in his memories that he forgot what they were doing out here. Glancing out ahead, he can't see much of anything, and he suddenly realizes that for all he knows, the ghoul rowing the boat could be taking them in circles.

"Ahoy, how much further?" he yells to the ferryman, but the ancient navigator just keeps paddling.

"What if we're lost?" Crom says, projecting a glowing grid onto the ether in front of her. "I can't tell where we are. This place has never been properly mapped."

"We're not lost," Adam says uncertainly as he climbs toward the front of the boat. "Ahoy, ferryman! Are we almost there?"

"Yep," the grizzled guide says, and Adam feels his feet slip out from under him as the boat crashes to a halt, sending everyone but its captain tumbling over the seats.

Looking back toward his students as he hoists his old soul onto the nearest bench, Adam announces, "We're here."

"Where's here?" Spuck asks.

"The deadland," Adam says, cold, wet, and tired like he hasn't been since he was alive.

The bleak shore extends endlessly in both directions, black water splashing over a beach of jagged gray stone. Clambering over the side of the boat, the class gazes upon the dreary landscape, and the ethereal lights surrounding the kids' humanoidesque forms fade dramatically. By some trick of the dark, the forest seems even further away than when they started out. Between them lies a vast wasteland, a seemingly endless stretch of cracked soil and dead things.

"*Aww*, how far is it?" D'ohry whines.

"Mmm, it's sort of hard to tell," Adam says, squinting across the dusty expanse. "Ahoy, ferryman!" he calls, but when he turns to reap some of the old skeleton's wisdom, the boat has already disappeared into the fog. "I guess we're on our own. How far could it be?"

Her aura growing dimmer by the moment, D'ohry says, "This is, without a doubt, the worst place I've ever been."

"I don't know," Ol' Garth muses as he buries his 'treasure' in the sand. "It has its charms."

"Ulch, why would you need to perform in-universe bodily functions?" the sparkly girl asks, and the cat scowls. "I know, I know… But I don't see what's so fun about *that*."

"Obviously you've never tried it," Ol' Garth says.

Looking out ahead, Spuck suggests, "There must be an easier way."

"Trust me," Adam assures the boy. "There's not."

Once they're convinced that there's no avoiding it, the kids come to accept their fate and reluctantly set out on the long march across the gray desert. The first few steps go okay, and then the complaining starts. Adam does his best to tune them out as they talk over one another in an endless chorus of groans and should-haves, but before long he finds himself grumbling right along with them. He simultaneously curses BM for getting him mixed up in all this, the kids for ruining his quiet afterlife, and most of all himself for letting them drag him along. The only one who seems to be having a good time is Ol' Garth, who's busy hunting little shadow creatures scurrying between the rocks.

"This is all Crom's fault," Spuck declares, wiping the dust from his shades. "If she hadn't given Mx. Buttmuncher the spitty idea, we wouldn't be on this so-called adventure."

"You're blam right it's my fault." Cromula flips her green hair in defiance as she tromps across the dirt in her big hiking boots. "If it wasn't for me, we'd still be stuck in class accessing ancient memory files. You should be grateful we get to be out here learning from a real space pirate."

"He may be a space pirate," Spuck says. "But if you ask me, he doesn't know spit."

"That's Asteroid Jones you're talking about!" Crom warns the boy, spinning around to face him.

"More like Plasteroid Jones," Spuck cracks and gives Ham a high five. "The guy spent half his life under the influence."

Crom's aura burns bright as she stomps toward him, her hand raised. "I'll give you five."

But before she can commence with her attack, Adam tells them, "Shhh, chut up a space second. Do you hear that?"

Listening closely, Ham says, "No."

"I thought I heard something near that bush over there," Adam says, pointing to a dry shrub gently rustling in the bitter wind.

"Now he's hearing things," Spuck says.

Adam listens for a moment longer and finally decides, "Yeah, maybe you're right. But let's try to keep it down. We don't want to attract attention."

"From what?" Crom asks.

"I don't know, and I don't want to find out." But when he turns back to take a head count, something seems off. "How many of you were there, again?"

"Five," one of them says. A small kid with scruffy hair and overalls, Adam can't seem to remember the boy's name. Pointing at them one at a time, he counts off, "Cromula, D'ohry, Ham, Spuckler, and me, Na-nu."

"Oh, right…," Adam says, embarrassed. "Well, we better keep moving."

As they continue their journey, he repeats their names in his head, so he won't forget – *Crom, D'ohry, Ham, Spuck,* and… The last one escapes him again, but when he glances over at the spastic kid, it comes back to him, and he harshly reminds himself that the one latching onto Crom's shoulders is, of course, little Na-nu.

# 16

"What about school?" I blurt before I can stop myself.

As Dad finishes loading our bags into the cargo hold, he assures me, "It'll be here when we get back. Anyway, we can only afford to go during the off-season. Are you sure you remembered to pack everything you need? Because we won't be back for two space weeks."

"Ye-es," I whine. "Stop asking."

"All right," Dad says. "But I don't want to hear any complaining when you realize you forgot the TV remote."

I scoff and fish the bulky rectangle from the front pocket of my overalls. "Like I would ever forget something that important."

"I was a chidiot to question you," he says as he obsessively rearranges the luggage in a quest for maximal spatial efficiency.

"That's what I keep telling you."

Standing back to admire his work, Dad glances at the time on his phone and asks, "Where's your mother? If we don't take off soon, we'll miss the weekend welcome parade."

I shrug.

"I'm coming!" Mom shouts as she fumbles her bags through the front door of the crumbling moon shack. Prancing across the moonscape in her newly-scrapped vacation sneakers, she drops her things in the dust and stares inside the cargo hold at the little parcel of space Dad left for her. "Where's all my stuff going to go?"

"That's what I'd like to know, Blev," Dad says. "I guess we'll just have to leave some of it behind."

"But I *need* it, Kren!" Mom cries.

"All right, all right," he says, winking at me. "We'll throw the rest of your stuff up front. Now, can we go already? I want to get to The Park while it's still light out."

Frowning, Mom smacks him on the arm and gathers her things. "He's just kidding," she tells me. "The days in Nü Park City last for space weeks, and there are rides and games and all kinds of fun things to do. I used to love going to The Park when I was a little girl."

"Don't forget about all the Park towns," Dad says, stepping around the side of the *Asteroid Jones*. "Every block is like a different imaginary seedy world brought to life."

"Shush!" Mom cries. "He's too young for that."

But it's too late. My imagination is already blasting off, and as we climb up into the ship, Dad winks at me again. The cabin smells musty, like the inside of an old moon shed. Between the cockpit and cramped living quarters, it doesn't take long to explore the whole thing. The only notable amenities are a lumpy foldout couch, the new space toilet, and an old fuzzy holo-tube.

As the junker takes off, I pull out my cot and drag it across the room to look out the porthole, when I get the sudden urge to abandon ship.

"Don't tell me you're splurging for starline tickets," Mom says as I step into the cockpit to break the bad news.

"Fish no," Dad tells her. "We're gonna travel the old-fashioned way, by black hole."

Her face scrunching, she asks, "Are you sure this old tub will make it?"

"Oh, she'll make it," he assures her.

They seem so happy that I just can't bring myself to tell them I forgot my shoes.

"*So…* how did you die?" Crom asks, waving her notebook.

Adam shrugs. "She didn't make it." Finishing off another Nü Guard, he tosses the can onto the side of the rocky trail, and it fades out of existence. No matter how much he drinks, he can't seem to get a buzz going.

"I'm tired…," D'ohry whines as she carries Na-nu across the gravel, her once-bright rainbow hair matted with dust and sweat.

Wiping his sunglasses on his faux tux, Spuck says, "We're all tired."

"Hey yeah, what's with that?" Ham asks, his mohawk drooping. "I've never felt like this before."

"It must be something in the ether." Crom pulls up her map, but she can barely navigate it with all the static. "It's messing with my ability to manifest."

Nodding smugly, Adam tells them, "This is another good lesson for you. In life, almost nothing works right, ever. And when it does, well that's what's known as a miracle." Another can of beer materializes in his hand, and he gulps it down with self-righteous satisfaction.

"But what about that beer you're drinking?" Ham demands. "There's nothing wrong with that."

Taking a long slurp, Adam smacks his lips and says, "This tastes like it was strained through a sweaty gym sock."

"Then why are you drinking it?" the pixelated boy asks, flickering angrily.

Glancing down at the shiny can, Adam shrugs. "What do you mean?"

"Come on you guys, things aren't that bad." Na-nu has become the group's de facto motivational coach, raising their spirits as they take turns lugging him across the endless desert. "Don't give up yet!"

Adam feels like they've been making good progress, but the dark forest is still impossibly far off, a black swell rolling over the edge of creation. It would be a lot easier just to quit now. But what would he tell Buttmuncher? *"Sorry BM, but those kids were just too dam annoying. I had to abandon them. Don't worry, they'll be better off with the rest of the lost souls."* He laughs to himself and when he's done daydreaming, he looks up to find the kids staring at him suspiciously. "Did I say that out loud?"

"No," Crom says. "But we can hear what you're thinking."

"Oh yeah…"

Dragging her flashing sneakers through the dust, D'ohry suggests, "I think we should just forget about this whole thing and go home."

"Now you're talking my language," Adam says. "This will be another important lesson – how to weasel out of things you don't want to do. But we have to make sure we're all on the same page. So, what do we tell your teacher? I think we should go with the old standby – I left the TV on. That's good enough, right?"

"Spit, I think so," Spuck says. "Let's get the fraiche out of here."

The class seems to be in agreement, but as they start to head back the way they came, Na-nu jumps down off D'ohry's back and cries, "What? No! We can't go back now."

"Why not?" Ham asks.

"Because," the kid says.

Moved by the boy's words, Adam says, *"Go on…"*

"Uh, because we have to keep going," Na-nu continues, the conviction in his voice rising. "Because it's the only way to go, and that means it's the way we *should* go. Otherwise, where would we go?"

In all of Adam's lives, he can't recall ever hearing such inspirational words. He can feel the call to adventure stirring inside him, and in that moment, he's prepared to follow Na-nu into the darkest, most horrific corners of the evil forest.

"Follow me and I promise to lead you out of this desert and to a new life," the boy announces. "As long as we keep going, we'll make it out. We just have to stay on the path. But we can't go back, because the only way forward is forward."

"Na-nu is right!" Crom says, with a renewed vigor. "It makes so much sense. I guess sometimes you just have to hear it out loud."

Something in the words cranks up the brightness on the kids' auras, and suddenly they're anxious to continue on their journey.

Even Adam feels like he's shed a few space years. His old joints have quit aching, and he starts to think that maybe the forest isn't so far off after all. "Well, should we get going?" he asks, stretching his arms.

Ham offers Na-nu a ride, and watching the little kid clamp his claws into the older boy's shoulders, Adam gets the feeling that they're going to reach the forest in no time.

# 17

"What are yuh s'pose tuh be?" the old scrapper asks, his gnarled fingers holding the candy bowl hostage as he waits for answers.

Swimming in Dad's old coveralls I tell him, "I'm Adam Carl Taylor, and he's Brinx James St. James."

"Never hert a yuh," the ancient humanoid grumbles, stepping out onto a mat with the words 'FISH OFF' printed in big bold letters.

"We never heard of you neither, mister," Brinx says, his head wrapped in a grimy bandana. "So, you gonna make with the candy, or what?"

The scrapper holds out the bowl, eyeing us suspiciously as we fish our hands inside. "*Just one.*"

But something is wrong. Instead of the familiar crinkly packages of the 'fun' size ration candies popular among residents of the Rental Belt, all we find are little pieces of cardboard.

Staring at his 'treat,' Brinx reads, "Ten percent off any purchase of twenty-five rations…"

"A coupon?" I ask, in disbelief. "That's it?"

"Hey, those are valuable," the scrapper says. "Took me a lot a work tuh cut 'em out. Even slicet my finger."

In a fit of rage, Brinx crumples the hunk of cardboard and throws it at the ackle's chest. "We're supposed to be the ones playing the tricks!"

Scratching his belly, the scrapper glances down at the discarded coupon. "I got canty corn…"

"Are you trying to kill us?" Brinx cries.

"Eh, git the fish outta here, will yuh?" the scrapper says, shooing us away from the door.

"Where's your Space Halloween—" Brinx yells, but the door shuts before he can say, "spirit?"

"Fish that guy," I tell him. "We got a lot of good stuff."

But Brinx won't let it go. Glaring at the busted door of the crummy moon shack, he digs through his garbage pail and emerges with a small cardboard box. With a mischievous grin, he flips open the lid to reveal half a dozen extra large marmalade crème eggs.

"Whoa…," Adam whispers. "Where'd you get 'em?"

"The Moon Mart had a bunch of irregular candy a few space months ago," Brinx says. "I've been hiding these babies in the back of my closet for a special occasion. I had a feeling they'd come in handy tonight."

We each pluck one of the sticky candies from its holder, and when Brinx gives the signal, we fling them at the scrapper's house. It's a gory scene as the eggs smash against the door, broken chocolate chunks and thick globs of crème splattering the unwelcome mat.

When we run out of eggs, we run back to the *Asteroid Jones* swinging our trash buckets and howling at the stars, when the door of the shack bursts open behind us and the scrapper screams, *"Yuh fraichin' ackle kids! I'll git yuh fer this!"*

As we climb into the *ship*, I urge Dad to take off before the scrapper has a chance to retaliate.

"I can't say I condone this behavior," he says.

"He tried to give us ration coupons!" I complain.

Dad thinks it over for a moment and finally decides, "I can't say I condone that either. But we should probably call it a night before you get us all killed."

Reluctantly accepting Dad's terms, we hurry back to the living room and dump our buckets out on the rug to admire our hauls.

"Wait," Brinx says, before we start digging in. "I got a surprise for the flight home." Rummaging behind the couch, he hauls his overnight bag onto the rug and pulls out a primitive-looking piece of hardware. "It's called a VCR. Ancient earthlings used them to watch videotapes. My brother scrapped it last space year. We even made a special converter so it'll work on modern holo-tubes. The movie I brought is like a fortieth generation copy, but you can still sort of tell what's happening." Once the player is hooked up to the old tube TV, he takes a plastic tape out of his bag and pushes it through the hinged door on the front. "I gotta warn you," he says as the display crackles and the distorted film starts to play. "They say if this one doesn't scare you, you're already dead."

"You died from a movie?" Crom complains between labored steps as they make their way across the deadland.

"Actually, it was the space hick whose house we crèmed," Adam says. "He shot us down with an illegal moon cannon."

"Hmm, I think I get it," she says, updating her notebook. "Always… eat… your… dessert."

Despite Na-nu's rousing speech, the long plod across the rocky desert has once again begun to take its toll on the class. Adam supposes they must be getting closer to the dark forest, but it's hard to tell. He's so tired he can barely lift his old legs, and the kids don't seem to be faring much better. For a while, they were loud and obnoxious as they suffered through their first muscle cramps and shoe pebbles, but now even their whining has ceased as their dead surroundings suck the divine spirit out of them.

When they approach what Adam deems to be a nice sitting rock, he tells them, "Let's stop and rest here for a space minute."

Without comment, his students slump down in the dirt. For a moment, Spuck looks like he's going to say something, but he can't seem to get the words out. The only one who's still in good spirits is Na-nu.

"Come on, guys!" the kid cries, bouncing around from classmate to classmate in his dusty overalls. "It's just a little further."

But glancing out ahead at the still-distant tree line, Adam is suddenly unconvinced. "Something's wrong. We should be closer by now."

"We're almost there," Na-nu assures them. "We just have to keep going."

"How do you know?" Adam asks. "We might end up walking on and on forever. In fact, I seem to remember there might be some sort of trick to it."

"Nah, there's no trick," the kid says. "We learned about this place in spirit school. It was lots of fun. Now, let's get up and go!" He scurries around the rock Adam is sitting on and hoists himself up on top of it. "I said let's go!"

Before Adam realizes what's happening, the little monster jumps off the rock and latches onto his back. Stumbling across the rocky soil, the old scrapper does everything he can to shake his attacker, but he's too old and too tired. As the desert begins to blur, he weakly claws at the kid's arms, but it's no use. He can feel himself fading, and suddenly the ground is rushing at him.

The next thing Adam knows, Na-nu's arms are being ripped away as a strained voice chokes, "Are you okay?" When the blurry figure comes into focus, he recognizes Crom's bright green aura leaning over him. "Don't worry, we got the little creep."

Turning his head toward a scuffle taking place nearby, Adam sees Spuck and Ham wrestling Na-nu into submission as the boy cries innocence. "How did you figure it out?"

"Easy," Spuck says, holding onto his sunglasses as the little devil squirms underneath him. "No one thinks school is fun. When he said that, I knew he was lying."

"Uh, I think school is fun," Crom chimes in.

"Yeah, but you're…" he trails off.

Patting the dust from her sparkly clothes, D'ohry asks, "How come we all thought we knew him?"

"He's a Dust Devil," Crom explains as she flips through her survival guide. "Though otherwise harmless, they are masters of deception, a skill they utilize to drain the energy of unsuspecting travelers."

"This little spit has been feeding on our spirits," Ham says, his image distorting with anger. "It's like that guy from the movie in your life."

"Dracula?" Adam suggests.

"No, that's not it," the boy says. "What's his name… Tommy Wiseau!"

"So, what do we do with him?" Spuck asks, struggling to hold onto the kid.

Checking her guide, Crom tells them, "It says here that the Dust Devil's greatest strength is also its greatest weakness. They're so good at lying that it's all they can do. To get the truth we just have to ask it the right questions."

"That's not true!" the little devil screams.

Glaring at the wriggling creature, Adam asks, "Are we going the wrong way?"

"No," it tells him with such conviction that he almost believes it. "I'm not lying."

"Why aren't we making any progress?" he demands.

"You are."

"How do we reach the Forest of Lost Souls?"

"Keep going."

"So we should go back the way we came?"

"Yes."

Even though Adam knows the kid is lying, he still wants to believe. Head spinning, he suddenly remembers, "There was something you said… 'The only way forward is forward.' So, that means the way forward isn't forward,

and if it's not back the way we came, then maybe it's…"
With his back to the tree line, he takes a step backward,
and Na-nu shrieks.

Shoving the other boys off of him, the little devil hops
to his feet and grins. "It was a lot of fun hanging out with
you guys. You're all really smart and krule." Spuck and
Ham lunge for the kid, but he dodges and, as if someone
hit fast forward, he skitters past them in a grotesque
backward crabwalk through the desert wasteland.

# 18.-20

The first thing I do as I step through the jerky automatic door of the cluttered warehouse is stop to smell the scrap. A funky mélange of alien odors from every corner of the cosmos, it's the stench of the universe itself.

"What the space hell is this chit?" Brinx asks, jutting his thumb toward a heap of shiny pots stacked where the comics used to be.

The clerk, a zit-faced teenager with a crackly voice, tells him, "It's not chit. That's high-quality copper cookware."

"But who's gonna buy it?" Brinx scoffs. "You think a bunch of broke scrappers are gonna plunk down the crits for a brand new stew pot? All they eat is rations!"

The clerk's shoulders droop, and he makes an expression like he's suddenly going to have to rethink his entire existence. "You could heat 'em up…"

"Would you guys come on?" Brinx's older brother, Doj, yells to us from across the aisle. "I told Mom I'd keep an eye on you." With thick ropes of green hair hanging to his shoulders, he's like a taller, cooler version of Brinx. "Help me find the air fresheners. I need a new one for my ship. Zindy said she won't fly with me until I do something about the smell."

Vaguely acknowledging Doj's pleas, we follow him down a long aisle packed with alien junk, daydreaming about the day when we're old enough to go out scrapping on our own.

"I'm going to have a theater on my ship," Brinx says. "The screen will be the size of the wall, and I'll have big comfy seats with cup holders that'll keep my drink cold."

"Well, mine's gonna have a whole movie library," I offer. "I might even let my friends borrow them. Maybe."

"Yeah, that's gonna be—whoa!" Brinx cries as he steps into the next aisle.

"What is it?" But I soon answer my own question.

There on the wall, next to the air fresheners and novelty sweat rags, is a glass case chock full o' videotapes.

"V-H-S...," Brinx moans.

Rushing across the aisle, we press our faces to the display case, grateful just to be laying eyes on the plastic treasures. My heart pounds and my hands shake as I scan the ancient relics of Earth's distant past. Most of them are loose, with titles hastily scribbled on their cases, while a few prize tapes include what are purported to be their original boxes. But that's only the tip of the junk pile. Videos in obscure formats from places I've never even heard of fill cases stretching all the way to the back of the store.

Overwhelmed by the scale of it, I ask Brinx, "Where do we start?"

"Right there." He points to a box so worn that the title is unreadable. All there is to inform us of the horrors contained within are the bulging eyes of a strange-looking creature reaching out from its dark basket.

"Whoa…"

"I have a feeling this is going to be the greatest movie ever," Brinx tells me.

When I wake from my video daze, I ask him, "How much is it?"

"Uh, says it's on sale for…" His face drops. *Two hundred crits?"*

"Aww, we'll never be able to afford that."

Once Doj is done picking out the stench they're all going to have to live with for the next space month, Brinx and I sullenly plod up to the counter after him with dashed dreams of videotapes spinning in our heads.

"Scrapper's Stank," the clerk notes as he rings up Doj's air freshener. "Good choice." As we're walking out, he places a sale sign in front of the mountain of copper cookware and sighs.

"Ninety percent off?" Brinx says. "Chit, I'll buy a stew pot. In fact, stew pots all around!"

"Turns out 'high quality' was something of an exaggeration," Adam laments as he hoofs it backward through the gray desert. "A quarter of the Rental Belt died of copper poisoning. What ever made that chidiot think getting rid of the comics would be a good idea?"

"A ponderous question," Crom says, writing in her notebook.

It hasn't been long since Adam and his annoying wards started walking in reverse, but they've already covered a lot of ground. They're close enough to the forest that he can hear the ghostly rustle of the trees in the distance, like the mad whisperings of the dead.

"When are you going to tell us about Pants Team Pink?" D'ohry whines, her bright sneakers flashing with every clumsy step backward.

Groaning, Adam says, "You know about *them?*"

"Sure we do," Crom says. "We're all Pants Team Pink."

"Of course you are." Even in death he can't get out from under their pink shadow. "Well, this is my life, and they don't come around until later. I don't know if we'll even have time to get to them."

"*Aww*," D'ohry moans. "But time is just an illusion. This field trip keeps getting worse and worse."

"I'll do you one better," Adam says. "I'll show you the time Brinx and I tried to sneak into the girls' locker room." But as he searches his miniature tape collection, he thinks better of it. "On second thought, I'd rather not relive that particular death. I don't think I ever fully recovered from what they did to us..." He trembles just thinking about it. "We didn't even see anything... much."

Shaking the dust from his mohawk, Ham suddenly turns to Spuck and cries, "Help Pants Team Pink!"

But before Spuck can answer the call, Adam puts his foot down. "No! There will be no theme songs on this adventure, especially not that one."

"Fine…," Spuck grumbles. Lifting his shades, he glances back over his shoulder and points behind them. "Is that something, or am I just seeing things?"

As she squints against the whirling sand, D'ohry says, "It looks like… an information desk?"

"It's probably just a mirage," Ham says, "like Jim Morrison and that weird naked Indian."

"Then why are we all seeing it?" Adam demands.

Scratching his pixelated head, the kid shrugs. "Good point."

Before long, D'ohry's assessment proves accurate, and as they back up toward the little sand-worn hut, she sticks her tongue out at the boy. "Told yuh."

When Adam reaches the counter, he spins around and is greeted by a grinning lesser demon with a thick leathery hide, its gray horns sanded down to the nubs. "Heading into the Forest of Lost Souls, eh?"

"Boy, hearing it out loud like that makes it sound like a *really* bad idea," Adam says.

"Well, you're in luck," the demon tells him, its cracked lips twitching. "This is the only place in Other Side where you can get a bona fide, dignified, country-fried map!"

"Oh, thank Rodney!" the old scrapper cries, the pain in his joints easing a little. "This is the first time all adventure that something is actually going right. And this map will take us all the way through the forest?"

"That's right," the demon says, and reaching into the ether, it produces a folded pamphlet labeled 'Map of Lost Souls.' "In there you'll find my special shortcut, guaranteed to get you there in no time."

Glancing back at the pack of misfits left to his care, Adam says, "You little chits have no idea how lucky you are to have a space pirate like me guiding you. There's souls who would pay a fortune for this kind of experience. Come to think of it, how much is this gonna cost me?"

But the demon bats Adam's concerns away. "All it'll cost you is one little death memory. A soul like you probably has plenty of 'em."

"Uh yeah," Adam says, clutching his tape bag. "I don't know…"

"Oh, come on!" Spuck shouts. "Just give him a boring one so we can get this over with and move on with our pre-lives, or afterlives, or whatever."

"Well…" Unzipping his bag, Adam lightly runs his fingers over the tapes, and the precious memories flash before his eyes. "Maybe I could give up just one. I wouldn't mind forgetting the time Bex Johnstone pulled my swimming trunks down in front of the whole gym class."

Trembling as it watches Adam painstakingly select the right tape to sacrifice, the demon suddenly snatches the collection with its bloody claws and howls. Thick gray spittle drips from the little monster's crooked mandibles as it tears at the bag. Adam can feel the strap slipping through his fingers, but just as he's about to lose his grip, a greater power intervenes.

With the kids' help pulling, they win the tug of war, sending the demon crashing back into its stall. It yelps and thrashes behind the counter and finally bursts out the back door.

For just a moment, as the monster lopes into the woods backward on all fours, its spell wears off, and Adam suddenly recognizes the little liar Na-nu staring back at him.

Frantically searching his bag, he shouts, "Some of my tapes are missing! That demon must have taken them."

"*What?*" Cromula wails. "How many?"

"I don't know," he says. "Some! A few, maybe half a dozen."

"Huh," Spuck says, brushing off his tux. "Spit, oh well."

"Not 'oh well,'" Adam barks. "We have to get them back!"

"Why?" the kid asks.

"Because they're my memories! They're the only ones I have, aside from all the other ones."

"Mr. Jones is right," Crom says. "Those tapes could hold the meaning of life itself. We have to go after them. What about the map the demon gave you? Maybe it can help us. Where is it?"

They desperately search the area surrounding the information stand only to discover that Ham has been gnawing on its crispy edges. "What, you mean this?"

"Yes!" Crom cries. "What does it say?"

"It's just a drawing of a smiley face with its tongue stuck out," the boy says, sucking the grease from his fingers. "But on the bright side, it's paper-lickin' good."

# 21

"The first thing I want you to do is collect all the rocks that are too big to rake." The doddering scrapper pads around the moonscape in his dusty slippers, muttering to himself as he examines the hunks of gray stone littering the yard. "But if it's a good rock, I don't want you disturbin' it. Just leave it where it is and rake around."

Brinx glances at me skeptically. "How do we know which ones are the good ones?"

"Here," the scrapper snatches a rock like any other from the ground and holds it up. "Look how ugly that is, all rough and lopsided. When you find one like this, I want you to walk it around back and gently place it on the pile."

Most space properties are equipped with a gravel pit, but as we follow the old coot around back, we're met by the largest collection of yard rocks I've ever laid eyes on.

"No problem," I announce, and taking the 'bad' rock from his hand, I toss it onto the shifting pile.

"I said *gently place it!*" the scrapper yells.

Glancing at Brinx, I ask the old guy, "Why?"

"Because that's the way I told you to do it! Now, come on." As he marches us back up to the front of the ancient moon shack, he points to a nearly identical lump of gray stone lying in the little patch of dead weeds he calls a lawn, and instructs, "Now, when you see a rock that nice, I just want you to leave it be. You got it?"

Lifting the moon barrow Dad loaned us, I tell him, "Just leave it to us. We'll have this place cleaned up in no time."

"Hmph, we'll see," the old man says, his chapped lips twisting as he sucks the life out of a sour ration candy. He continues to glare at us for a few long space seconds and finally shuffles back toward the house.

I can already sense Brinx's resolve fading as he pokes the rocky soil with his rake, so I say to him, "Don't worry, soon we'll be witnessing horrors the likes of which most people in this universe have never seen. Just keep reminding yourself that it's only a job, only a job, only a job…"

"I heard you the first time," he says.

Kneeling down in the moon dust, I grab one of the uglier rocks and hoist it into the barrow, when I hear the old scrapper shouting, "I told you, leave the good ones where they are!"

For the remainder of the afternoon, Brinx and I haul rocks according to the particular demands being barked at us from the porch. By the time we finish transporting the last load, our fingers are blistered and bleeding, and our spirits are thoroughly broken. I don't even care about the crits anymore. All I can think about is getting the fish away from the old ackle before one of us makes him choke on his sour candies.

It's hard to make out exactly what he's yelling when I toss the last rock onto the pile, but as the mountain of moon rocks comes tumbling down over us, it sounds sort of like, *"Gently…"*

"Don't you ever get hurt from all this dying?" Crom asks.

"Of course," Adam says, exasperated from the memory. "If it hadn't been for the relatively advanced medical techniques available at the time, by my last murray there wouldn't have been much of me left. Plus, you can't see the emotional damage. Rocks still sort of scare me."

The forest howls as the class makes its backward approach. Ancient gnarled treethings covered in black bark rise up through the ether toward a shadowy canopy that's little more than an idea shrouded in black mist somewhere far above their heads.

"This is where the tracks end," Crom says, marking her map. "Na-nu must have taken the tapes inside."

Her rainbow hair having lost most of its luster, D'ohry peers into the dark and whines, "You mean we have to go in *there?*"

"And thus you have learned another crucial lesson," Adam lectures. "Never, ever, under any circumstances, lose my stuff."

"It's not our fault that stupid demon got its claws on your tapes!" Spuck argues.

"Nevertheless." Peeking his head into the darkness, Adam reminds himself that he can still blame this all on BM if any of the kids get lost or go insane. "We must fulfill our mission to retrieve my property."

"And find Daizy…," Crom reminds him.

"Oh right, that too."

Lifting his sunglasses, Spuck whines, "But how the fraiche are we supposed to *see* in there?"

"*Fish.*" Adam mentally curses himself for not thinking of that sooner, and the kids glance at each other dubiously. "My powers are useless here. Can't one of you manifest a flashlight or something?"

"None of our powers work either, remember?" Spuck glares at the 'teacher' as he pulls a useless rubber steak out of the ether. "The only way we're going to get through this is by accident."

"What about you?" Adam says, looking at Ol' Garth.

The cat concentrates for a moment, and a bowl of raw Morlock appears next to him. With a shrug, he proceeds to scarf the simulated monster meat.

"Let me give it a try." Closing her eyes, the aura surrounding Crom's soul flows down through her arm and into her hand. When enough energy has accumulated, she forms a ball of divine light with which to banish the shadows. Still, it's only bright enough to give them a vague idea of their surroundings as they step between the trees.

Blindly stumbling into the greater unknown, the darkness quickly becomes so complete that it feels alive, and before long Adam glances back to find that the gray light of the deadland has been completely snuffed out.

"We're never going to make it like this," Spuck whispers, his voice quavering.

The kid is right, of course, but Adam doesn't have any better ideas. "Dam that Buttmuncher. If it weren't for that chidiot angel, I could be back at the house enjoying a fine *Nightbreed* right now."

"Uh guys," Crom says. "I don't want to alarm you, but I can't keep this light going forever."

The orb in her hand dims slightly, and Adam cries, "Why didn't you tell us?"

"Isn't it obvious?" she yells.

"I thought so," Ham says.

The darkness seems to be taking a sick pleasure in their plight. Adam can feel it mocking them as whatever terrible creatures it holds prepare to tear their souls apart.

Yelping as the shadows nip at his heals, he screams, "What are we gonna do now?"

"I for one vote we go home and forget all about this stupid adventure," Spuck says.

"Me too," D'ohry concurs.

As the orb of light shrinks down to half its original size, they unanimously scramble back the way they came, tripping over giant roots and other shadow things.

Adam can almost see the terrible creatures circling them just beyond the light's reach, and he moans, "This is just great. Not only is the light running out, it's probably attracting every monster in sight. Are you sure we're going the right way?"

"I think so," Crom says. "But we turned around so fast, we might have veered off course."

"We're going to die before we ever got to live!" D'ohry says between loud sobs.

Huddled inside the dim glow of the dying light, the kids hang onto Adam as if their souls depended on it. Pale and shaking, they remind him of his life.

For a moment, the fear slips his mind, and he asks them, "Hey, did I show you the time I missed the ship home from school?"

"*What?*" Spuck looks up at the old scrapper, and his face scrunches. "We're about to be wiped out of existence, and you want to show us another one of your noid deaths?"

Adam shrugs, and somehow it's enough to convince them to gather inside the faint haze of his memory as the darkness closes in.

# 22

"Okay, I'll show you, but you can't tell anybody," Mr. Dorxly says, anxiously tugging on his dusty sweater vest. "I'll get in big trouble if anyone finds out."

"Phh," Adam scoffs. "Who do you think you're talking to?"

"Yeah," Brinx says. "We're cool. Come on, we stacked all the chairs and swept the whole room. That was the deal."

"Okay. But no touching." Glaring at them mistrustfully, the AV teacher reaches into his desk drawer and emerges with something so incredible that I hardly believe my eyes.

"Whoa, it's even got the original box…" I instinctively reach for the movie, but Mr. Dorxly snatches it away.

"What'd I say?" He waits for me to put my hands behind my back and then sets the tape down on the desk in front of us.

"*Surf Nazzies Must Die*," Brinx reads, squinting at the worn cover. "What's a surf nazzie?"

"I don't know," I tell him. "But there's only one way to find out. This school has centuries worth of outdated video equipment. Let's pop it in."

But just as suddenly as they were raised, our hopes are dashed when Mr. Dorxly stuffs the tape back inside his desk. "Are you crazy? We can't play it."

My heart sinks. "You mean you've never watched it?"

"Of course not," he says. "It's an antique. Even if by some miracle the image hasn't completely degraded, I would never risk harming it."

"Then what's the point?" Brinx demands.

Scoffing, the teacher says, "If you don't get it, then there's nothing I can do for you."

His refusal only increases my curiosity, but before I can come up with a sufficiently pitiful plea, the last voice a space kid in this school wants to hear calls from the door behind us, "Mr. Jones, Mr. Bartly!" And as if by some authoritarian magic, Brinx and I start mumbling apologies before we even know what we did wrong. "What are you two still doing here?" Mrs. Sparx demands.

"Uh…" I glance at Mr. Dorxly and he gives me a warning glare. "We were just asking Mr. D about NTSC and PAL ancient Earth analog video formats. It turns out the different frame rates resulted in a slightly altered viewing experience. See, while NTSC displays at 29.97 frames per Earth second—"

"Enough," Mrs. Sparx growls, her top lip peeling back to reveal a sharp set of canines. "You've really done it this time. All the ships have already left. How are you going to get home?"

As we wait in the parking lot for my Dad to show up, I can't help but think we're wasting precious time that could be better spent finding out what's on that tape. If I could only come up with the right combination of words to convince Mrs. Sparx of its educational value, I'm sure she would come to see things our way and overrule Mr. Dorxly's fuddery.

Readying myself to deliver the most persuasive rant of my life, I finally turn to the vice principal and blurt, "Us learn from watch video!"

Mrs. Sparx looks down at me like she's worried my brain just fell out of my head. "Huh?"

"Hey, here comes… something," Brinx says, pointing at a dark object approaching the dome. "What is that?"

"Well, it's not a ship," Mr. Dorxly says. "But if it was anything to worry about, the emergency system would have been triggered by now."

As the emergency alarm wails, I shout, *"Can we go watch the movie now?"*

*"Yeah,"* Brinx says. *"I wanna find out who the surf nazzies are and why they must die, while* we're *still alive."*

*"Movie?"* Mrs. Sparx growls, her thick pelt bristling as she turns her wrath on Mr. Dorxly. *"I warned you to stop filling these kids' heads with that mindless junk. If we survive this, I'm confiscating all contraband from your classroom by rule of educational forfeiture!"*

Turning toward us, Dorxly yells, *"I told you not to tell anybody! Now none of us gets to watch it. Are you happy?"*

Shrugging as the stray moon rock hurtles toward us, I shout, *"Not particularly."*

"I never did get to see that movie," Adam laments.

"What was the purpose of seeing that?" Spuck complains, huddled next to the rest of the kids inside the soft glow of Crom's light.

"The purpose," Adam says, "is to teach you that you're doomed if you do and you're doomed if you don't. Sometimes in life the only sensible thing to do is sit back and enjoy the show while you still can."

"How is that going to save us?" the boy asks.

"It won't."

"Then why are we learning about it?!"

"To keep our minds off the constant threat of annihilation closing in all around us," Adam says, the hot breath of some invisible pointy monster panting down his neck. "That's most of what life is all about."

The kids whimper as the orb in Crom's hand makes one final attempt to hold off the encroaching dark before finally flickering out. As the light fades and the darkness envelopes them, Adam breathes the ether in deep and awaits the inevitable rending of his soul. But it never comes.

"This isn't so scary," Ham finally says.

Once the old space pirate's eyes adjust to the lack of blinding light, he realizes there's nothing in the dark but a bunch of petrified twigs and harmless ghouls. Glancing back the way they came, he can even see a hint of gray light peeking through the trees.

"This one is so cute!" D'ohry squeals, her sneakers flashing as she chases a moaning phantom through the ghost wood.

"Hey, there's a trail over here," Crom announces. "This one's going on the map. I'll call it the Ghost Trail."

"Very original," Spuck cracks, and nudging Adam, he says, "So all that whimpering and doom talk was just to scare us, huh?"

"Uh, of course," the old space pirate lies. "I always knew we were in no real danger. Anyway, we better keep moving. Those tapes aren't going to find themselves. We'll take the Ghost Trail. Let that be another lesson – where there's a road, there's a way, or something."

Defying the malevolent influence of their dark surroundings, they start down the trail with renewed spirits. Apparitions haunt the ether, aimlessly floating between the trees and across the narrow path, and every once in a while, Adam catches a glimpse of Ol' Garth pouncing on one of them out in the mist beyond the edge of the trail. But for the most part the flitting spirits pay no attention to the foreign travelers as they wander deeper into the woods.

After a short while, despite the fact that they haven't left the path, Adam begins to worry that they missed a turn somewhere, or that there's some trick to it like in the deadland. Following his fear down a series of irrational cognitive byways, it's not long before he finds himself questioning his entire afterlife. Positive that he's gotten them all lost, and that everything is hopeless in general, he panics and spins around to see if walking the trail backward will make any difference. But he doesn't get more than a few steps into his experiment before crashing into the backs of his students, stopped dead in their tracks.

Momentarily losing his runaway train of thought, he asks, "What's the holdup?"

"There's something in the way," Crom says.

"So, walk around," Adam complains, and making his way to the head of the class, he finds a small ghost sleeping in the path.

As the lost soul lazily wakes from its slumber, he nudges it back into the trees, and they continue on their way. But soon, the fear returns. This time he's convinced they're being followed. He can feel eyes crawling across his back, but every time he whips his head around to confront the stalker, there's no one there. Still, he can sense that something is out there, something evil just waiting for its chance to burst out of the shadows.

"You're not going to make it," a cold voice suddenly whispers into Adam's ear, and he yelps.

But when he looks back, all he finds is the ghost that was sleeping in the trail, and he asks it, "Did you say something?"

"I said you're not going to make it," the ghost tells him. "You're lost."

"No we're not," Adam argues. "I mean, I don't think we are."

"Oh, you're lost all right," the ghost says. "You don't even know how lost. That path you're on, it never ends, just goes on forever."

"It does not," Adam says, uncertainly.

"Does too."

Glaring at the lost soul, he tells his students, "Ignore it. Just keep walking and it'll go away."

The old scrapper tries not to look back as they continue down the dark path, and for a while he succeeds.

But with no sign of anything but more trees ahead, his curiosity soon gets the better of him, and he glances over his shoulder to find the ghost trailing close behind.

Losing his brule, he cries, "*Grahh*, stop following us!"

"Why should I?" the ghost asks.

"Whatever," Adam tells it. "I don't care. We're just going to keep walking."

"Go ahead," the ghost says. "But you're still not going to make it."

# 23

The class can barely contain themselves, their raw kid energy practically exploding out of them as they race toward the entrance of the holo-theater. As one of the only things to do in the Rental Belt, most of them are frequent viewers, but there's something about being there in the middle of a school day that gives the whole experience an extra thrill.

*"No running!"* Mrs. Sparx growls, startling innocent day watchers as her voice booms out over the parking lot.

Dorxly was supposed to take us, but she didn't trust him to pick out something educational. Part of the deal for getting out of class is that we have to see an ancient alternate Earth documentary called *Demolition Guy*, or something. But Brinx and I have other plans. It so happens that on this very morning, the theater is showing an ultra rare print of *Friday the 13th: Part III* in full holo-modified 3D, and we're going to see it.

"We're supposed to meet him around back," Brinx says, doing everything in his power to avoid Mrs. Sparx's attention, "at the 'door with no knob.'"

"When?" I ask.

"Now."

*"Now?"*

While Mrs. Sparx is busy snapping at the rest of the class to get inside, the two of us slip out of line and make a mad dash around the side of the building.

With my back pressed up against the moon brick, I ask, "Do you think she saw us?"

"I don't know," Brinx says, huffing. "I don't think so."

"You two!" the vice principal howls, and we both freeze. "Quit fooling around and get inside. I'm warning you, Bimmy Jinx, if you make me miss the previews, you're going to spend the rest of the space year as my personal pooper scooper."

It's the first time I've ever been glad that Bimmy is such an ackle. Before Mrs. Sparx has a chance to notice we're gone, we hoof it around the back of the cruddy parking lot until we come to a knobless door surrounded by cigarette butts. Composing himself, Brinx knocks out an odd pattern, and the door unlocks.

"What is that?" I ask.

Grinning, Brinx says, *"Come-and-knock-on-our-door..."*

The door opens a crack, and a dark-eyed kid with semi-translucent skin pokes his head out. "You bring it?"

Brinx nods, and reaching into his backpack, he pulls out a holographic Chibi-Sitcom card in a hard plastic protector.

"Wait a space second," I cry. "You're giving up your ultra rare first edition Little Ritter 'Red-Eyes Day Tripper' variant?"

Brinx shrugs. "I never liked that show anyway."

Basking in the card's awesome reflective foil, our usher steps aside, and we walk past him into a dark hallway full of backdoors.

*"Which one is it?"* Brinx shouts over the clashing movie sounds echoing through the corridor.

But the kid won't take his eyes off the card. *"How should I know?"*

*"Come on,"* I tell Brinx, pointing at the big block numbers stamped on the doors. *"It's theater eighty-two."*

Racing around behind the screens, we finally find the right door and slip inside just as the movie is starting. I can't believe we got away with it. As we slump into our flattened seats at the back of the theater, we nervously glance at each other and burst out laughing.

We can hardly contain our excitement for what we're about to see. But as the lights dim and the conspicuously explicit credits begin to roll, it quickly becomes apparent that we're at the wrong movie.

"Rat farts!" Brinx says. "We must have got the time mixed up."

"Should we leave?" I ask as holographic globs of naked alien flesh are projected onto the ether.

"Yes," Brinx says.

But neither of us moves.

"I don't know what I'm watching," I tell him, as acts of carnality so far removed from my understanding as to defy everything I thought I knew about the fundamental laws governing the universe play out all around us. "But I can't look away."

"It turns out sometimes the ratings are there for a reason," Adam says. "The movie was of course retconned from my memory when my life was reset, but I was never quite the same after that. Some things you just can't unsee."

Scoffing as he kicks a dead branch into the shadows surrounding the dark path, Spuck says, "It didn't seem so scary to me, just really gross."

"Well…" The old scrapper mulls it over for a moment. "Things are more complicated in-universe. There are endless annoying layers of context and meaning surrounding everything. It's a whole thing. It's a lot more real when you're living it."

"Sounds exhausting," a wispy, detached voice butts in. "Lucky for you it was your last life, since you're not going to make it."

Adam glances back and juts his thumb out at the smiling spirit floating at the group's heels. "No one asked you." But he's secretly beginning to worry that the disembodied pest may be right. They've been walking through the ghost wood for what feels like an eternity, and they still haven't come across a single sign of life.

"I bet it's lying," Cromula says, her green ponytail bouncing in the dark up ahead. "Just like Na-nu."

"No I'm not," the ghost says.

"Let's test it," Adam suggests. "I've got the perfect question. Of the endless string of direct-to-video *Hellraiser* sequels, which is the best?"

"Phh, I can answer this," Ham says.

The ghost's face scrunches, and it finally says, "I don't know what you're talking about."

Shooting the little ghoul a suspicious glare, Adam tells it, *"Good answer..."*

*"It's true,"* D'ohry suddenly wails, holding her face in her sparkly hands. "We're never going to get out of this forest. Soon we're all going to look just like that... *thing*!"

"She's right, you know," the ghost says. "You're not going to make it. You're already lost. Once you're here long enough, you'll end up just like all the other ghosts haunting these woods."

"I think I see something," Crom mercifully interjects, pointing toward a dark luminescence spilling out onto the path up ahead.

"Don't look at that," the ghost says, floating in front of them and waving its stubby paws. "That's nothing."

But the wispy spirit proves powerless to stop them as they charge through its spectral body and race down the path. When they reach the source of the dark light, they discover that it's emanating from two crackling globes of black flame suspended in mid-ether. The floating torches serve as guideposts at the end of a worn trail branching off the main road. Beyond lies more darkness, but it's accompanied by a sound so familiar that Adam would recognize it anywhere.

When the ghost catches up to them, it says, "There's nothing down there for you. If you take that trail, you might never find your way back."

"What, are we going to get *more* lost?" Spuck asks.

"He's right," Crom says, marking the trail on her map. "The only way to find out what's in the dark is to look."

"Maybe we'll even get lucky and run into the fishing demon that stole my tapes," Adam suggests.

Despite the ghost's protests, it follows close as they cautiously step past the flames. Coarse chatter and tortured howls echo through the ghost wood as they make their way toward a shadowy structure in the distance. A lone goblin grunts at them contemptuously as they pass, but when it notices the ghost trailing behind them, it keeps its distance. After a short hike, they come to their dark destination – an ugly establishment torturously hewn from the black trees that surround it. Reaching branches weave around the outer walls to form a twisted lattice which Adam supposes must require constant pruning.

Before they get too close to the building, the old scrapper pulls the kids over to the side of the trail and warns them, "We have to be careful in there. We don't want to look too conspicuous."

"How do we not do that?" Ham demands.

"Here…" Adam tosses his halo into the woods and grabs a handful of dirt to muddy their faces. "That's worse, I guess. Just try to act unnatural."

"This is so humiliating," D'ohry whines, stomping her flashing sneakers in defiance.

"Humiliation is one of the cornerstones of life," Adam lectures, raising his finger as they try to blend in with a group of beasts plodding toward the entrance.

When they enter the soggy hut, all glowing eyes turn toward them, and in the local parlance, Adam grunts, "Aha, we were just-"

"Hey!" the demon behind the bar growls, motioning toward the lost spirit floating behind them. "You can't bring that in here. You'll spook my customers."

# 24

The night sky is bright with the ancient light of a bajillion stars. The way their reflections bounce off the still surface of the black water makes it feel like we're suspended somewhere in between, casting our poles out into deep space.

"Isn't Mom going to wonder what happened to us?" I whisper, trying not to disturb the delicate rhythm of the thousands of invisible alien insects chirping all around us in the cool, unfiltered air.

Gradually reeling in his line, Dad says, "Nah, I told her it was gonna be a long haul. It's not every space day you get the chance to go night fishing on Sproing. This is one planet in the United Empires I'd consider moving to, if we were the richest scrappers in space…"

Both of us turn quiet as my bobber sinks beneath the surface, but before long it pops back up with nothing on the line. "I don't get it. Why would anyone pay that much for an old moldy alien costume?"

The dark silhouette sitting across from me shrugs. "I guess it was used in some ancient Earth abduction documentary – *Third Encounters*, or something."

A soft breeze suddenly blows across my skin, like a gentle caress from the universe itself, and as I soak in the night air, I tell Dad, "This is a great time."

"Ooh, I almost forgot!" he says, jumping out of his seat. "I got us something special." The boat rocks beneath us as he rummages through the cooler where we keep the glow worms and moon cheese, and he soon emerges with two shadowy cylinders. Cracking the cans, he hands one over and says, "I figure you're old enough now to have a beer. It's against UE regulations, but what isn't? And anyway, there's nobody out here to arrest us."

We clink our cans together, and I eagerly gulp the golden beverage. But as the yeasty liquid hits the back of my throat, I reflexively spit it back out, spraying the boat with suds. The whole lake goes silent for a moment, and we both lose it.

"S-stop," Dad pleads between loud bursts of laughter. "You'll s-scare all the f-fish."

"I c-can't h-help it," I stammer as I roll off the back of the bench.

After our shared fit has petered out, I hear a strange noise coming from the other end of the boat, and when I lift myself up, I find Dad's dark figure hanging off the side, wrestling with my pole. Stumbling over our gear, I grab onto him, and we both yank as hard as we can. For a moment it looks like the line is going to snap. But somehow it holds, and we manage to wrestle the beast to the surface, grasping blindly into the dark water to pull up the biggest Cursing Crapper ever recorded in Sproingian waters.

"If we hadn't caught the evidence, no one would believe us," Dad says, with a tired laugh.

Thrashing around the bottom of the boat, the crapper yelps, "*Ack... ack, ack...*"

Exhausted, I hunch over the bench and whimper, "It must have been the beer."

As we lay laughing alongside our prize, I get the distinct sensation that this is one of those times I'll always remember.

Once the adrenaline wears off, and I can hear something besides my heart pounding in my ears, I notice a soft hum coming from above us.

Looking up into the sky, Dad yells, "You're not taking it!" And I whip my head up to find a glowing saucer hovering over our boat. "We caught this fish fair and square. *Finders keepers!*"

The ship responds with an odd honking melody, and before we can get out of there, our boat is consumed by a brilliant flash of light.

The clingy ghost looks in longingly from the other side of the window as Adam downs what's left of his tarry grog and slams the empty mug on the table. "It turns out the chidiot quantum kid we sold the costume to was just trying to scare us, but he accidentally reversed the polarity on his tractor beam and vaporized our boat instead."

The ghouls and gargoyles surrounding him fall into hysterics, splashing their drinks and tumbling onto the floor laughing.

"I went fishing once," a gaunt demon with small black eyes and a mangled nose announces, and the howls die down as everyone at the table turns to look at the pitiful creature. "Fraiche, that was a good life…"

"Well, I call bullspit," one of the monsters growls.

Without looking to see who said it, Adam juts his thumb toward the other end of the table and turns to order another drink from the bar. But before he can say Sour Soul Stirrer, a large hairy paw grabs his shoulder and spins his frail spirit back around.

The hulking beast, its red eyes burning underneath a pair of stubby horns, leans down and says, "My last life, I was born in the United Empires. I went on vacation to Sproing every space year, and I never heard of no Asteroid Jones, or Adam Jones, or Kren Jones neither. Everyone knows it was my granddaddy Zlorp what caught the biggest crapper in those waters. What do you say to that, holy boy?"

"Aha, I say your granddad was obviously a skilled angler." Adam groans, bending under the crushing pressure of the monster's powerful claw. "But no matter how big his catch was, ours was bigger." He prepares himself for a goring as a ravenous scowl forms on the beast's face.

But instead of sinking its teeth into his divine spirit, the monster laughs. "You're all right, for a holy man."

The jovial growling resumes as the beast returns to his table, and Adam lays his spinning head on the bar. It's been a long time since his last night out, and his tolerance isn't what it used to be. Even so, he's having the time of his afterlife. He seems to remember there being something he's supposed to do, but when the bar demon returns, the thought slips his mind, and he orders another couple drinks, one for each hand.

He's just gearing up to party for the rest of eternity when a small voice calls out, "Ahem."

He turns to find Cromula staring up at him with an accusatory scowl, and his shoulders slump. "Oh yeah…"

"So, did you find your tapes?" she demands.

"Um, not yet," he says, sipping his grog. "But I will. Just go play in the arcade for a little while."

"What do you think we've been doing this whole time?" Her green aura burns bright, attracting the unwanted attention of some of the monsters seated nearby. "We didn't come all this way to watch you get wasted. This is supposed to be a learning experience, remember? Anyway, only one game is working."

"What is it?"

"What do you think?" she growls. "The claw machine. But it's rigged. It never grips hard enough. It just steals your energy."

Thinking back to the long space days he spent skipping school at The Park, Adam says, "I used to be the space king of the claw machine. Maybe I should give it a try, or twenty. Here, hold my beer."

"No!" she cries, ripping the glass from his hand. *We have to find the tapes.*

"Right, right, the tapes…," he muses, sipping his other beer.

As they mull over their options, Adam's beastly new friend wraps his thick arm around the scrapper's neck and whispers, "I like you, holy boy, and I want to help you out." He points his giant index finger at a little chubby devil seated at the end of the bar. "I overheard you say you're looking for some memory tapes. I happen to know that demon found hisself something just like that."

"Holy spit," Crom says. "Those have to be your memories. But how do we get them back?"

"Just go talk to him," the monster advises. "I'm sure you'll be able to come to an arrangement. In the meantime, I'll help your friend unrig the claw machine."

"I don't know about this," Crom says as Adam snatches his grog back from her and slugs it down. "What are you going to offer him?"

Sporting a thick sludge mustache, he tells her, "I don't know. But I can tell it's going to require my most persuasive powers of persuasion."

As he waves to the bartender, she asks, "What are you doing now?"

He shrugs, reminding himself that she's still new to all this, and patiently explains, "Getting another beer."

# 25

Dad's face twists inside his helmet as the hand truck he's pushing crashes into a small moon rock and spills a crate full of scrap into the dust. My helmet is tuned to *Music from The Drew Carey Show*, so I can't hear whatever he's yelling at me as I collect the slightly damaged cargo and load it back onto the stack. We gradually make our way back to the *Asteroid Jones*, wading through the corporate detritus that litters the crummy dump moon, and when the ship is loaded, he smashes his hand against the button to close the cargo hold door. As soon as the room is repressurized, he rips his helmet off and starts angrily mumbling at me.

Tapping the side of the bubble surrounding my head, I mouth, "I can't hear you." But the taunt just enrages him, and he jumps on me, yanking at my helmet until he finally pulls it off. "What the fish is wrong with you?"

"We're supposed to be a team out there!" he shouts. "One rock almost ruined a whole day's work, all because you weren't doing your job. You have to start paying more attention. This time it was just some dented hardware, but a mistake like that could cost us our lives."

"Do you think I did it on purpose?" I cry, fueled by a general sense of frustration with the universe. "It was an accident!"

Suddenly, we're rolling on the ground wrestling in the scrap, when Mom opens the hatch and yells, "What's going on back here?"

"*Nothing…*," Dad and I moan as we take our hands off each other and conspicuously brush off our spacesuits.

Stepping through the doorway, she briefly looks us over and starts pawing through the latest haul. Dad stomps out of the room, grumbling, and once he's gone, she glances back at me. "You did a really good job today."

"Thanks," I say. "But he's right. I messed up."

Setting down the busted electric ration opener she was looking at, she wraps her arms around me. "I know you'd rather be back at home with your friends. But what you're learning out here is going to help you for the rest of your life. Your dad is only tough on you because it's a tough universe out there. In his own way, he's trying to protect you. We both are. It might not seem like much now, but one day you're going to look back and miss all this."

"I doubt it," I tell her, sniffling as I blindly reach into one of the crates and grab what turns out to be a battered UE softball. "Why does he have to be such an *ackle*?" I whip the ball across the room, and guided either by my rage or an incredible stroke of unluck, it bounces off the wall and hits the cargo hold door opener, dead center.

Staring into his dark grog, Adam says, "It's the only time I ever actually hit what I was aiming for."

"*Ahaha*," the short red demon sitting on the stool next to him croaks and smacks his little paw against the bar. "You're one bad spirit. Even I never killed my whole family."

"It was an accident!"

The demon waves his hands and winks. "Hey, you don't have to tell me. I've had a lot of *accidents* in my lives."

"I'm not lying!" Adam whispers, lest any of the other monsters get the wrong idea.

"Me either." Leaning in close, the demon says, "Anyway, fair is fair. But I don't keep the tapes on me. We'll have to hike out to my camp to watch them. It's not far."

Adam sacrifices a small piece of his soul to the bar to pay for their drinks, and he follows the wobbling devil to the door. But before he steps back into the cold dark ether, he suddenly remembers his class.

He finds them in the arcade, huddled around the claw machine and calls, "Ahoy! I think I found my tapes."

"Come on baby…" Ham says, his soul flickering as he moves the control stick in a strange pattern and taps the button on top. The machine's mutated fingers wrap around a rubber gargoyle, and the kids cheer as the claw drags the stretchy monster kicking and screaming over to the prize slot.

Taking over the controls as Ham fishes the creature out of the slot and tosses it onto a growing pile of gruesome novelties, Spuck says, "We're going to stay here for a while, at least until this thing is out of prizes."

"Fine," Adam says, throwing his hands up in defeat. "But don't go anywhere. This shouldn't take long."

"You better come back for us," D'ohry cries. "I don't like the looks of some of these demons."

"Well, I'm coming with you," Cromula announces, buttoning her travel vest. "Someone has to look after you, and I don't want to spend the whole adventure stuck in this cruddy bar."

"What about you?" Adam asks the cat curled up on top of the claw machine, but Ol' Garth just shrugs and makes himself more comfortable. On his way out, the old scrapper turns and tells them, "We'll be right back…"

"Wait, I want to thank that demon for helping us unrig the machine…" Crom says.

But the big beast is nowhere to be found.

They find the little devil waiting outside, but it bristles upon seeing Crom. "Who the fraiche is this?"

"Don't worry, she's brule," Adam assures the demon. "She's my… spiritual adviser."

The devil looks Crom up and down and finally relents. "Whatever, just stick close, and stop acting so lively. If you're not careful, you're going to attract the wrong kind of attention."

As the demon leads them away from the bar, Adam tries to telepathically coordinate a plan with Crom, in case anything goes wrong, but there's too much interference in the ether. Laughing nervously, he tells her, "This reminds me of the time my girlfriend and I went on vacation in the woods and got attacked by a Kandarian demon."

Crom scoffs. "That doesn't sound real. Are you sure that isn't from one of those movies you're always watching?"

"Could be…" he says, getting tangled in the cobwebs of his mind. "I also remember getting sucked into a giant rift in space time and saving the universe. So, you're probably right."

Maybe it's the moaning of the ghost wood or the lost souls startling him every time he turns his head, but Adam is seriously beginning to despise BM. If he still had all his memories, he'd turn around right now and give the angel holy space hell. But things being as they are, he has to come up with a way to get his tapes back without losing his soul.

"So, supposing I like what I see, what would it take to get you to let go of these treasures of yours?" Adam asks.

Glancing back at the scrapper with a lecherous smile, the devil says, "I bet I could come up with something. You look like you got a head full of porno."

"What?!" Adam cries. "I do not. Who told you that?"

Shrugging, the demon says, "I calls 'em like I sees 'em."

As Adam tries to figure out what the fish that's supposed to mean, the ruddy runt stops dead in its tracks and looks around to make sure they weren't followed. When their unholy guide is satisfied, it steps off the path and disappears into the shadows of the surrounding woods.

"You're sure we can trust this spitiot?" Crom whispers.

"Fish no," Adam says. "But I think I can take him…"

Poking its little horned head out of the trees, the demon asks, "You coming, or what?"

The old scrapper glances at Crom, and lifting his palms, he sighs, "I guess so…"

**26-37**

Lugging my backpack through the rowdy halls, I feel like I'm carrying the weight of the universe on my shoulders. I do my best impression of myself arriving on any other dreary school day, but as I scurry through the kid war zone, narrowly skirting Bimmy's detection, I can hardly contain my excitement, or fear, of what lies within. More valuable than everything I've ever owned put together, I can feel the forbidden object's dark power tugging at me.

When I reach my locker, I nervously swipe the lock screen, but my shaky finger keeps messing up the combination. I breathe a sigh of relief when it finally clicks open, but before I can stow the precious cargo inside, something yanks at my bag, and I immediately shift into defensive mode. I spin around, smacking my head against the locker door, only to find an amused Brinx chuckling at the pain which he has so unnecessarily wrought.

"So, did you bring it?" he asks, broadcasting his excitement to the whole school.

"I don't know what you're talking about!" I announce, and lowering my voice to a whisper, I tell him, "But yes, I brought it."

Brinx's eyes light up, and he reaches for my bag. "Come on, lemme see."

"Okay, okay, just be brule!" I tell him, nodding toward the snarling lycanthrope headed in our direction.

We try to act casual as Mrs. Sparx walks past, but I smile a little too enthusiastically, and she gives us an accusatory growl. Once she's out of earshot, I reach into my bag and pull out a dirty balled-up t-shirt. Glancing around to make sure no one is watching, I carefully unwrap it, and for a long moment all we can do is stare, hypnotized by the same indecipherable image that first mangled our imaginations.

"I can't believe it's finally ours," Brinx says, lightly touching the deformed fingers of the monster on the tape's faded cover.

"And it only took us four space years to save up enough crits," I note. "We should put it away before anyone else sees."

But the macabre allure of the tape is so strong that we can't take our eyes off it, and as we gaze at the fragile treasure, a familiar annoying voice asks, "What's on the tape?"

Before either of us can respond, the video is snatched out of its swaddle, and we spin around to find Bimmy clumsily inspecting the precious object. Not knowing any better, he holds the box upright, and the tape nearly slips out.

"It's nothing!" I shout, and jumping into action, I wrest the movie from his grubby fingers.

"Is it one of those videotapes you guys are always talking about?" he asks.

"No," Brinx says. "I mean, yes…"

"Oh cool." Lingering for a moment, it suddenly becomes apparent that the bully isn't planning to attack us. "You think I could watch it with you guys?"

"Fish no," I instinctively respond. "You're just going to do something to ruin it."

"Yeah, whatever," he says, and for a moment, he looks almost hurt. But then he laughs, flashing us his crooked grin. "But there's only one tape and two of you. So, who gets to keep it?"

Brinx slowly turns toward me, and he suddenly grabs the tape. "I practically killed myself for this movie!"

"So did I!" I wail, holding onto the other end.

Any hopes of keeping our prize a secret disintegrate as the other kids gather to watch the tug of war.

With the box bending under our sweaty fingers, Brinx yells, "You're going to ruin it!"

"No you!" I shout back.

Responding to the commotion, Mrs. Sparx comes bounding down the hall, howling, "You boys stop that right now!"

I can feel Brinx's hold slipping, but just when I think I've won, he lets go, and the video goes flying out of its box. All heads turn to watch the plastic rectangle spin through the air, and the world slows to quarter speed as the tape, and our hearts, shatter on the dusty tile.

"It cost us a dozen murrays to learn our lesson," Adam laments. "But eventually, we got to watch the movie. *And it was good…*"

"So, who ended up keeping the tape?" Crom asks.

Just in case the trees are listening, Adam lowers his voice. "We decided to split it. Brinx took the movie, and I got the box. That way neither of us could resell it for full value without the other."

"Oh… but then Brinx got to watch it whenever he wanted."

"No, because…" Thinking it over for a moment, Adam says, "Hey, you're right! That sneaky son of a… Well, I guess it doesn't matter now. Plus, he was the one with the player."

Fumbling through the dark, the only clue to where they're going is the sound of the little devil's feet tromping over dead leaves a short distance ahead of them. At the speed it's moving, Adam decides the old rumors must be true – demons *can* see in the dark.

"Hey!" Crom calls out. "I just realized, I think we finally lost that annoying ghost. I don't see its aura hanging around anywhere."

"Thank Rodney," Adam says.

"Shhh!" the demon scolds.

"Sorry."

The further they travel, the more jumpy Adam gets, flinching at every moan and bloodcurdling howl that echoes through the forest. Imagining the things that must be causing the other things to make those noises, he gets ready to grab Crom and get the fish out of there, when he spots a dim flicker in the distance. At first he takes it for a trick of the dark, but as they move closer, he recognizes all the accoutrements of a small campsite — a ratty tent, damp sitting logs, and a crackling gray fire.

"I was beginning to think you were full of chit," Adam tells the demon as he enters the camp and warms his aching hands over the ghostly flames. "Now, where are those tapes?"

"They're right over here," the demon says, its shadow stretching as it sidles around the fire. "But first, I'd like to take another look at that big collection of yours."

Tugging on Adam's arm, Crom whispers, "I think we should get out of here."

"Nonsense," the scrapper tells her. "Just let old Asteroid Jones take care of this." Turning to the demon, he says, "Listen, I don't want this to get physical, but it's the two of us against the one of you. I may look old, but my soul is still spry, sort of."

"Who said there's only one of me?" the demon asks.

Before Adam can figure out what in the space hell the little devil is going on about, a large paw lands on his shoulder, and he glances back to find his beast friend from the bar looming over him.

"Oh good!" the old scrapper says. "You can help us teach this demon a-" But when he notices Crom's impatient glare, he gradually comes to acknowledge the reality of their situation. "Oh…" Taking a closer look at the campsite, he suddenly realizes that the big rips in the waterlogged tent are actually claw marks, and that the dark, goopy liquid splattered across the leaves isn't bean juice.

He winces as the beast digs its jagged claws into his shoulder and growls, "Those were some nice memories you showed us back at the bar, the kind demons kill for."

The monster grins wide, showing off his jagged soul munchers. "Now, why don't you hand over the tapes?"

"And you'll let us go?" Adam asks, hopefully.

But the hairy demon just laughs and shakes its giant head. "I'm afraid not. I mean, I'm not afraid. You're the ones who should be afraid."

"Just hand 'em over," the little creep says. "And maybe we'll go easier on you than we did this loser."

The devil juts its thumb into the air, and Adam looks up to find a familiar lesser demon hanging from one of the black branches. Grinning nervously, its childlike face covered in dark bruises, it says, "These guys are really great. They've been treating me real well. We're all *real* lucky to be kidnapped."

# 38.-71

"*This way!*" Brinx cries over the endless howling sandstorm that shrouds the surface of planet Abraxas.

I nod and we make a break for it across the open desert, our krillsuits filtering the sparkling sand particles out of the air as we breathe. When we find a good spot to call the great glow worm, I crouch down and put my hand to the ground to feel for its presence.

"*Nothing,*" I shout.

Brinx lifts his finger, and rummaging through his knapsack, he emerges with his phone. He taps at the glass and then turns it so I can see.

"*That should do it,*" I tell him.

Cranking the volume, he presses the phone's speaker to the sand, and the ground reverberates with the slapping bass of the *ALF* theme. After a few space seconds, a pained shriek pierces through the storm, and Brinx and I take off across the dunes as the ground shakes beneath our feet. Soon the glimmering hide of the ancient creature breeches the surface. For a moment it looks like we're going to be worm food, but just as I'm about to tumble backward into its giant maw, Brinx holds his tinkling phone up to the great annelid, and the monster sinks back under the sand. As the iridescent mass swims past us, we each latch onto its segmented body with our safety harpoons, and using the method demonstrated by the instructor, we run out in a wide arc and swing up onto the beast's back.

Once we get our bearings, Brinx celebrates with the tourist battle cry, "*Wee!*"

"*Ahaha!* All hail the masters of Abraxas!" I announce.

With the warm wind whipping across our faces, we ride the worm all afternoon, until Brinx's phone finally receives a warning that if we're not back in fifteen space minutes we're going to be charged for another session.

When we get back to the rental hut, we trade in our krillsuits and head out to the parking lot to wait for our rides.

"That was so brule," I tell him as we wander across the empty lot. "Thanks for paying. Next time, it's on me."

"Yeah, next time…" Brinx says.

We talk about girls and videotapes for a while, and soon his brother shows up, impatiently honking before his ship even touches down.

"I guess I'll see you in school," I tell him.

Brinx looks like he wants to say something, but he can't seem to get the words out. Finally, he blurts, "I'm not gonna be at school anymore. We're moving."

"*Wha?!*"

"My dad got a new job dust farming for the UE," he says. "I wanted to tell you sooner."

I don't know what to say, so I don't. We stand there in silence for a few space seconds, until Doj lays on the horn.

As Brinx runs to the ship, I raise my hand, and he yells back to me, "*I left you something in your bag. You're my best—*" But the rest is drowned out by the wind, and a few moments later, he's gone.

Before long, Mom arrives in the *Asteroid Jones*, and I climb up into the passenger seat.

"So, did you have a good time?" she asks.

As soon as I look at her, I start sobbing, and she does her best to console me as we take off for home. On the way, I rummage through my bag for a consolation ration, when I discover Brinx's gift – a familiar plastic rectangle stamped with the letters 'VHS.'

"Aww, so he left you the tape after all?" Crom says, her green ponytail falling up toward the dark ground. "Spit, how many times did you two die together?"

Laughing, Adam says, "I think it was something like… thirty-four."

"Wow," Crom says. "He must have been a really good friend."

"Yeah," Adam sighs. "He really was. We hung out a few times after that in the virtual world, but it wasn't the same, and eventually we just grew apart. You know how it goes."

"No I don't," she says.

"Well, you will."

"I'm a good friend," Na-nu says, and Adam and Crom turn to glare at the lying lesser demon hanging upside down from the branch next to them.

Wriggling under the strings of demon saliva that bind him, Adam shouts, "You're the whole reason we're in this mess! As soon as we get out of here, I'm going to—"

"Would you guys scut up?" the little red demon growls as it spreads Adam's video memories out in front of the gray fire. "We're never going to let you go, so you might as well get comfortable up there."

"You already have my tapes," Adam complains. "What do you need us for?"

The giant horned beast he briefly called friend clomps toward the prisoners and inhales the dim glow radiating off them. "You two are an unlimited source of divine energy. Once your spirits are broken, we're going to feed off you for the rest of eternity."

"*Aww*," Adam moans.

"But why'd you string *him* up?" Crom asks, swinging in Na-nu's direction.

The hairy demon snorts. "He's just really, *really* annoying."

"I am not," Na-nu says.

Stomping back to his rotting ghost wood log, the beast says, "See? Even he knows it."

"I mean, how could he not?" Crom says.

The red devil salivates as it counts the tapes, running a bloody claw across their cases. When it finds one it likes, it plucks the plastic rectangle out of the carrier and gets lost in the memory.

"What is it?" the beast asks.

Willing itself out of its nostalgic trance, the devil grins wide and says, "It's death. They all are."

"Gimme one!" The beast growls, and snatching a tape from the bag, it shudders, "*Ughgh*, it hurts so good."

"Look how many there are," the devil says, gazing at the collection. "I told you that little spitiot would be useful. It's a good thing I made him tell us where he found those memories he was peddling."

Adam and Crom turn toward the evil kid hanging next to them, and he grins. "I didn't not not tell them."

"Would you stop lying for five space seconds," Adam barks.

Thinking it over for a moment, Na-nu says, "Yes."

"You gotta check this one out," the devil tells its partner-in-pain as they exchange videos. "The kid accidentally vaporizes himself cleaning out the exhaust on his family's cruddy spaceship. It's brutal."

The captives hang around as the demons psychically probe Adam's tapes. For a while, they grunt and holler loud enough for the whole forest to hear as they indulge in his agony. But it's not long before they descend into a deep binge hole the likes of which not even the strongest of demons could escape.

"Do not underestimate the power of the tapes," Adam lectures. "They're as dangerous as they are educational. But this should buy us some time. Now how the fish do we get out of here?"

"We could try singing the *Pants Team Pink* theme song," Crom suggests.

"How will that help?" Adam asks.

"It'll make me feel better..."

Groaning, he asks Na-nu, "What about you? Don't you know any demon tricks that can help us?"

"I sure do," the evil kid announces.

"Well, let's hear them," Adam says, skeptically. But as they stare back at him, blank-faced, he remembers Na-nu's 'ability.' "Oh, right…"

As the demons space out on Adam's memories, he focuses all his concentration on manifesting one last beer, but his powers are useless.

"What was that?" Crom suddenly cries. "I thought I heard something."

"Maybe we'll get lucky and our spirits will get ripped to shreds by some shadow creature," Adam says. "At least then I won't have to worry about my tapes."

"I'm serious," Crom says, and he glares at her. "I know, I know, so are you. But just listen."

Under the sound of the crackling fire and the demons' gratuitous moans, Adam can just make out the irregular crunching of dead leaves in the woods behind them.

"Play another one of your deaths," Crom pleads. "You can access them from here, can't you?"

"Maybe," Adam says. "But I'd have to project it the old-fashioned way, with my mind, and that requires a lot of effort."

*"Please,"* she whimpers as eternal annihilation closes in around them. "Pick a fun one."

"A fun death…" He laughs, but when he notices that even Na-nu is trembling, he's again reminded that they're both just kids, and that none of this is their fault — it's BM's. As the dark threatens to snuff out what little life remains in the flickering flames, he tells them, "Sure, I got a fun one for you."

# 72-73

As we pull through the crusty airlock of the old dome, I can already tell that this isn't going to be any fun at all. "Why can't I go scrapping too?"

"Because it's too dangerous where we're going," Mom claims as she brings the ship in for a landing. "You wouldn't have any fun stuck out there with us anyway."

"You're gonna have a great time," Dad says. "You used to love coming out here when you were younger. I wish I could stay here with you. But this is the biggest scrap of our lives. After this, we can finally get out of the Rental Belt. Chit, if things go really well, we might even be able to move on-planet somewhere." He squeezes Mom's hand, and she squeezes back.

Unbuckling myself from the kiddie seat, I scurry to the front of the ship to look out over the junkyard below, and I suddenly start to feel like staying with Grandpa might not be so bad after all. There's a space pirate's bounty in old scrap to explore in the front yard alone. Plus, it means

I won't have to spend my vacation at home. It hasn't been the same since Brinx moved away.

As we lug my bags down, I breathe in deep and glance back at Dad. "Does it always smell like this?"

"Yep," he says, sniffing the musty recycled air. "It really takes me back. This place has had the same air filtration system since *I* was a kid."

"Is it safe?" I ask.

Dad thinks for a moment and shrugs. "I think so…"

While the yard is mostly comprised of dead weeds and gravel, I do spot a few patches of green sprouting up around the scrap as we navigate the cluttered moonscape.

"Ow!" Mom cries, tripping on some crumbling ship part. "Is he ever going to get rid of this stuff?"

"I don't think so," Dad says.

The house is like something out of an old horror movie. A parody of an ancient Earth Victorian built from scrap, the crooked, peeling structure is an anachronism from a place and time that never existed. When Dad rings the doorbell, a loud gong sounds from within, and soon the door creaks open. As we stare into the dark entryway, our host suddenly bursts out onto the porch flailing his arms, his chest covered in bright red goop. With a dramatic moan, the old man slumps to his knees and crashes at our feet.

After a moment, I stick my finger in the red syrup covering his shirt and touch it to my tongue. "It's strawberry."

"Okay…," Dad says, setting my bags down. "We'll seeya in a couple space months."

"Hey, I'm dying over here," Grandpa complains.

We share a long hug, and Mom makes me promise to take care of the ancient space pirate as we say our goodbyes. After we watch them take off, Grandpa helps me bring my stuff inside. Compared to our little moon shack, the place is huge. It's been space years since I was last here, but it looks just like I remember. The design is a bizarre mash-up of alien styles combined in such a way as to produce a distinct sense of 'old.'

"You can have the room upstairs," Grandpa says, as I explore the main hallway. "I thought you might like to stay in your dad's old room. I'm almost done fixing it up. But for tonight, you can sleep on the couch."

The old man leads me into a cluttered den at the end of the hall, and I'm instantly overwhelmed by all the old books and alien scrap scattered around the cozy room.

"You don't say much, huh?" Grandpa says. "Well, that's okay. I'll heat us up some rations and we can watch a movie."

My interest is suddenly piqued. "Movie?"

"Yeah, you know," he says as he fixes up the couch. "It's like a story that you watch. You can pick one out."

Before I can question him further, he leads me to a dark closet across the hall, and once he locates the light switch, the ancient bulb flickers on to reveal the old man's movie cave – a wall-to-wall, floor-to-ceiling collection of videotapes, discs, and chips from around the universe.

"If only Brinx were here to see this…"

"Sure, I can get us some drinks," Grandpa says, shuffling off down the hall.

I don't know where to begin. There are more videos than I could watch in two lifetimes, although the horror section is seriously lacking. Rummaging through my backpack, I grab my tape and search for a spot to add it to the collection.

As I climb up the wall, reaching toward a place of honor on the top shelf, Grandpa pops his head in and asks, "You pick something yet?"

But before I can even begin to know how to answer, my foot slips, and the universe comes crashing down on top of me.

Whatever is skulking in the shadows is getting closer, but the chidiot beast and its devil companion are oblivious, hunched over the colorless fire below, lost in memory as Adam, Crom, and Na-nu hang from the trees like live monster bait.

"I'm gonna miss you guys," Adam says. "I know we haven't been together long, but you kids have been like an annoying sitcom family to me. I'm even gonna miss Na-nu, to a much lesser extent."

The child demon's lips quiver, and black tears drip up its evil little face. "I'm not gonna miss you either."

Unable to contain himself any longer, Adam sobs, "That's the nicest thing you've ever said to me."

"Stop talking like that," Crom says, her voice quavering. "You have to have f-f-fai—" But before she can get the word out, she starts bawling right along with them.

The sound of their suffering is enough to wake the devil out of its trance, and it jumps to its feet, frantically searching the campsite. "What? What's happening? I mean, I like what I'm hearing, but we didn't even start torturing you yet."

"Our souls are all going to be annihilated and everything is hopeless," Adam wails.

"Oh…" The demon yawns and glances around the camp. "Is that all?" With a tired sigh, it plops back down on its stump and reaches for another tape, when something makes a loud rustling noise not far from the campsite. "What the fraiche was that?" Scrambling past the fire, the devil kicks the sleeping beast in the leg and cries, "Get up, you big oaf."

Stretching long and deep, the hairy monster scratches its demonoid nether regions and says, "I was having the best death. I was out playing in the yard when I accidentally uncovered a nest of space hornets. It was so slow and painful…"

"I forgot about that one," Adam says.

"Would you get off your big argh?" the devil complains. "There's something out there."

The beast climbs to its hooves, and squinting out into the darkness, it bellows, "Whatever it is will stay out there if it doesn't want its soul ripped in two."

Something crunches the eons' worth of packed litter just beyond the dwindling light of the gray fire, and for a moment, as they wait for the unknown monster to pounce, even the demons seem scared. Adam figures their only hope is to pray that the monster prefers dark souls and takes mercy on the rest of them, but that hope is shoved into the meat grinder with the arrival of a familiar black cat.

As Ol' Garth traipses through the camp, he glances up at the hanging prisoners and then at their demon captors and asks, "What are you spitheads looking at?"

"You ever try cat soul?" the beast asks.

Grinning, the little devil shouts, "*Grab it!*"

But before they can get their unclean paws on Adam's loyal pet, the beast takes a plastic lycanthrophant to the face. The demons curse into the darkness as they search for whatever threw the bloodsucking pachyderm, when they're hit by a sudden torrent of cheap novelty horrors. While the demons are defending themselves against the onslaught of souvenirs, Ol' Garth bounds back into the woods, and as soon as they get the chance, they stumble after him.

Once they're gone, the leaves behind the captive souls start rustling, and as they brace themselves for annihilation, four familiar spirits poke their heads out of the trees.

"What took you so long?" Adam demands upon his disciples' approach.

Climbing up on one of the logs to tug at the saliva ropes binding the scrapper's arms, Spuck says, "You're lucky we found you at all."

"You can thank Ol' Garth for that," D'ohry tells them, as she dissolves Crom's spit ropes using nothing but common holy powder. "When we couldn't find you, he caught the trail of your… *unique* odor." Looking down at the crud on her sparkly fingers, she cries, "Ew! Is this spit?"

"What about *him*?" Ham asks, jutting his pixelated thumb at the lesser demon kid hanging alongside them. "Should we leave him here?"

"Yes!" Na-nu cries.

"You heard him," Adam says, but when he considers all the fear-induced bonding they've shared, he reluctantly reconsiders. "Nah, let him down. He's not so bad, once you accept the fact that every syllable he utters is a lie."

By the time they've all been freed, the fire has gone out, and they stumble around the campsite in the dark, searching for a way back to the path.

"I think this is where we came in," Adam says, feeling along the wet logs.

"Are you sure?" Crom asks. "If we go the wrong way, we could get lost for… *ever*."

Somewhere close by, Spuck asks, "Which way?"

"Where the fish is Ol' Garth when you need him, again?" Adam moans.

"I'm right here."

"Finally," the scrapper says. "Now, how do we get the fish out of—"

But he loses his train of thought when the fire suddenly flares up, filling the campsite with gray light. The demons grin as the big one holds Ol' Garth over the flame. Adam hurls holy expletives at them, but just as he's about to launch a feeble attack to rescue his cat, something holds him back.

"I caught him," Na-nu says, cheerily. "This proves I'm one of you."

Turning toward the lesser demon hanging off his arm, Adam growls, "You little spit!"

74

School break with Grandpa turned out to be more fun than I expected. Most mornings were spent in front of the TV, watching ancient Earth sitcoms and eating cold rations in our underwear – when the bimonthly supply ship made its rounds, he even let me pick the flavors. The days were for exploring all the weird scrap scattered around the lawn and throughout the many cluttered rooms of the dust-caked house. Then at night, after the old man passed out, I'd stay up late downloading obscure horror movies and banned cartoons. But while it's been a nice place to visit, I sure as chit wouldn't want to live here.

"*Breakfast!*" Grandpa calls. "You want mush or paste?"

When I've finished packing, I drag my bags into the hall and hurl them down the steps, nearly taking out the old man waiting at the bottom.

"Aright, aright," Grandpa says. "I'll take the paste."

"Sorry," I tell him as I clamber down the crooked staircase and snatch the tray of meat mush out of his hand. "I didn't see you there. I'll eat mine outside."

"Are you sure?" he asks, waving his chopsticks. "Your parents aren't gonna be back for a while yet. Plus, *Dobie Gillis* is on."

"I saved a bunch of shows on my remote. I'll watch them when I get home." Swinging the big door open, I kick my bags out onto the porch and wave goodbye.

"Aright," he says as he lifts a glob of purple paste to his mouth. "But you don't know what you're... ooh, that's good."

As I sit on the front stoop, shoveling down my mush, I begin to wonder what school will be like without Brinx around. Things are never going to be the same, but I'm beginning to think they might be o-kay. After my short stay in Misery Acres, I feel ready for a new start.

I gaze out at the stars for a long while, trying to spot the *Asteroid Jones* as it comes in for a landing, and eventually I doze off. The next thing I know, I'm jerking awake to the sound of Grandpa's phone whistling "The Fishin' Hole." I suddenly get the sense that I'm missing something, and searching through my bags, I'm horrified to discover that I almost forgot my most prized material possession.

Pulling the heavy door back open, I dash down the hall and yell, "I forgot something."

But when I glance inside the den to see what the old man is watching, the look on his face stops me cold, and I forget all about my tape.

Ghostly pale, his eyes red and full of tears, he ends the call and looks up to find me standing in the doorway. "Adam…" he chokes. "I'm so sorry."

"A few pieces of the old ship were all that was ever recovered," Adam says as the memory fades.

"So, what happened?" D'ohry cries, sparkly tears streaming up her forehead. "Did you ever find them again?"

"I thought about going to see them after I used up all my murrays," he says. "But by then, I was a different person. None of us could go back. Not really."

Setting the tape back down on the pile below, the red devil shudders, "*Ughuhuh*… that's the stuff."

The kids whimper as they hang upside down from the petrified branches of the ghost wood. Fresh out of saviors, Adam figures if they were doomed before, now they must be double doomed. The demons even managed to catch Ol' Garth, whose soul is currently being slow roasted over the gray fire.

"You guys are so dead," the cat says, cackling as the flames singe its fur. "You don't even know."

"I know one thing," the beast says, tossing another log onto the fire. "You're gonna be good eatin'."

Na-nu sits shivering atop one of the wet logs at the edge of the camp, trying to fool himself into believing his own lies. "I'm a good boy. I did the right thing. Everything I do is good…"

"Aw, don't put yourself down like that," the little devil tells the kid. "I admit, I hated you at first. But you proved yourself by helping us catch these argholes. If it wasn't for you, they might have gotten away before they ever got to taste true suffering. You're one of the worst demons I know, and your treachery will not go unrewarded. Since you are responsible for all this misfortune, you can have first dibs."

"No fair!" the beast growls. "Why should we let this lesser spithead take what's ours?"

Stepping in before the hairy monster can bring its big hoof down on Na-nu's skull, the devil says, "Because he's one of us now, and we want to keep our golden boy happy, at least until his luck runs out."

"Fine, but the old man is mine." Baring its giant fangs, the beast stomps across the camp, and with one swipe of its claws, it cuts Adam down from the tree.

His hands tied behind his back, the old scrapper wriggles in the dirt, powerless to escape, when Na-nu shouts, "*Wait!*" All eyes turn toward the lesser demon as he nervously glances around the fire. "I can't eat in front of other demons. I get nervous."

"Oh, come on!" the beast groans. "This is ridiculous." But when it looks for guidance, the little devil just shrugs. Pointing to the sobbing kids hanging in the trees, it says, "What about them?"

"Uh, well…," Na-nu says, digging the toe of his sneaker into the dirt. "They don't count, right? They're just livestock."

The burly demon stares at the kid for a long moment and finally says, "I like the way you think. But make it quick, and don't violate them too much. But if you do, clean up before we get back."

Grinning and nodding like a deranged puppet, Na-nu says, "You got it. You guys are really kind."

As if stung, the devil says, "Watch your mouth!"

Na-nu waits for his fellow demons to shuffle off into the woods, and once they're gone, the evil kid leaps down onto Adam and starts gnawing at his chest.

"*Arghh,*" the scrapper wails.

"Get away from him, you spit!" Crom cries.

Adam wriggles and howls in imaginary agony, until he realizes that the kid's teeth aren't sinking into his divine flesh but into the saliva ropes wrapped around his wrists. Once the strands are weak enough, he uses his old soul strength to break out of his bonds.

"But why would you help us?" he asks as they get to work freeing the others.

Na-nu shrugs. "Because I really love the demons back there, and I don't want to see their bones ground into holy powder. I'm not feeling guilty about handing you over to those spitheads either, if that's what you're thinking."

Crom screams as the little demon latches onto her and starts biting through her ropes, but before long, she's back on unhallowed ground. Once the rest of them have been gnawed loose, Adam tries to manifest a treat for the demon, but all he can manage to pull out of the ether is a handful of stale candy cigarettes. Na-nu happily accepts the expired sugar sticks and chomps them down with black tears in his eyes.

"Let's go, before the chitheads get back," Adam instructs.

"Him too?" Spuck asks, wiping the spit off his fake tux.

"Of course he can come," D'ohry says. "He just saved all of our souls."

Looking the demon kid over, Spuck says, "I still don't trust him."

"Fine," Ham tells his friend as he peels the spit off his flickering arms. "You can stay here and think it over."

"On second thought," Spuck decides, "I'm suddenly beginning to like the little spitiot."

With that decided, they noisily creep toward the edge of the camp, when Adam hears a familiar and desperate *meow*. "Oh chit!" he moans, glancing back toward the fire. "I forgot Ol' Garth."

Waving the others on, he hurries back to the fire and starts tearing apart the strings of spit binding the cat's paws. As soon as the his pet is free, Adam says, "Now, let's get the fish out of here."

"What the fraiche is this?" a small but evil voice suddenly cries, and Adam turns to see the demons stepping into the firelight.

Slashing at the sticky remains of the saliva ropes hanging from the ghost wood, the burly demon roars, "I've had enough of this spit!"

Before Adam has a chance to escape again, the beast leaps over the fire and sinks its jagged teeth into the old scrapper's shoulder. For a few frames, he's too shocked to scream, but when his senses finally catch up with him, he cries out from a pain unlike anything he's experienced since he was alive. It feels just like...

# PART 11

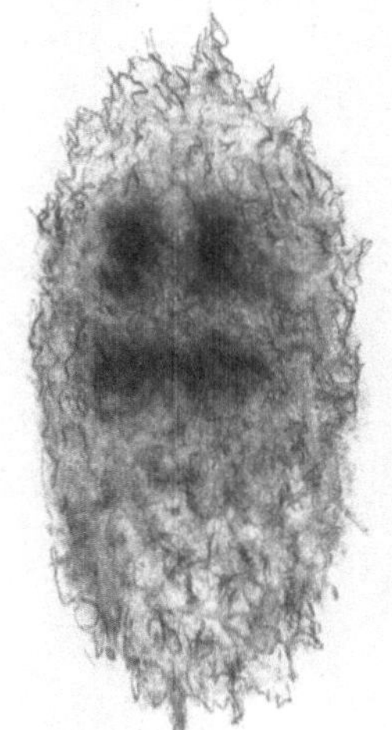

# Death

75

My universe is one of darkness. Its dimensions are the exact height, length, and width of the inside of my head. It is a cold and unforgiving place, full of invisible monsters that feed only on fear and regret. They are eternal and insatiable, with the power to snuff out even the brightest of lights. This place offers no consolation, no answers, no hope. The only comfort I receive comes from its sameness, which I wrap around myself like a cold, wet towel.

I know there are people and places and life outside the shadows, but they are too distant and vague to be of any importance, like the mumbling, scripted prattle of a TV left on in another room.

The harder I struggle, the deeper I sink into the void, until the life I used to know seems like little more than a pleasant dream. I try to hold onto it, but I can feel it fading, and as the remnants dissolve into the ether, a crack forms in the darkness.

I'm assaulted by a bright slit of light shining into the room as Grandpa calls, "*Adam?* Are you alive in there?"

Squinting against the bright intrusion, I pull my pillow over my head and groan, "No."

But the old man either doesn't believe me or doesn't listen. "I warmed up your favorite ration – special dark flavor. Or is that my favorite?"

"Just leave it by the door," I grumble.

I can hear him enter the room and set the tray on the nightstand. Sitting on the edge of the bed, he lays his hand on my shoulder. "You don't have to eat it. You can stay in here as long as you want. But when you're ready, I've got a surprise for you out in the yard."

After he leaves, I fall into tears, both out of hatred toward the universe and love for the ones who brought me into it. I sob until I'm too exhausted to think, and once I'm all cried out, I stare into the dark for what feels like space hours.

At some point, I hear a deep growl coming from the shadows, and I begin to fear that my despair has summoned some terrible cosmic monster. But as my awareness shifts back into my body, I realize that the sound is coming from my stomach.

The aroma from the blackened ration next to my bed makes my mouth water, and I finally give in, groping for the tray in the dark. I gobble it down like it's my first meal, and when I'm finished, I'm surprised to find that I feel a little better. Grandpa even left me a ration pop, which although melted, really hits the spot.

Summoning a strength I didn't know I had, I throw my legs over the side of the bed and push myself up. They're wobbly, but they manage to carry me out into the bright hall and down the stairs. When I reach the den, Grandpa is nowhere to be found, and I suddenly remember him saying something about a surprise.

I find the old man outside hauling part of the remains of the *Asteroid Jones* across the dead lawn. As soon as he sees me, he drops what he's doing and cries, "You're up!" Waving for me to follow, he leads me toward a big pile of spare parts and what looks like the beginnings of a new old ship. "I figure there's almost enough scrap out here to build a whole 'nother junker. We might have to order a few parts, but if we work hard, we'll have you flying by next space year. So, what do you think?"

I can feel the tears coming back, and as Grandpa wraps his arms around me, my heart bursts.

Cold and shaking, Adam wakes from his delirium and asks the green-haired girl cradling him, "Am I dead?"

"Well yes," Cromula says. "But no more than you were before."

A bolt of pain shoots through him as he touches his finger to the torn flesh surrounding his throbbing shoulder. "What happened?"

"Stay back!" Spuck shouts, and Adam twists his head to find the young soul splashing holy water at the demons who stole his video memories.

"That arghole demon tried to suck the divine energy out of you," Crom says. "We managed to rip you away before it could do too much damage, I think. But I could barely make out that last death. You just kept mumbling something about spaceships and ration pops."

Pacing the edge of camp, the beast growls, "That water won't last forever. When you run out, I'm going to tear your souls apart, starting with you."

The monster turns its fiery eyes on Na-nu, and the child-like lesser demon yelps, "What'd I do?"

"You let them go!" the little devil cries, glowing with rage.

"They tricked me," Na-nu lies. "I wouldn't help them on purpose. I'm one of you! Everyone knows you guys are the baddest demons around."

"*Ackkk!*" the devil shrieks. "Stop saying nice things!"

As soon as Adam's head quits spinning, Crom helps him to his feet, and they join the rest of the kids cowering behind Spuck. The old scrapper desperately searches for a way out of this mess, but their chances of survival are dwindling with every splash of glistening water from Spuck's canteen. As hopelessness sets in, the old space pirate's shoulder screams.

Snatching the canteen out of the boy's hand, Adam tells the class, "Get out of here."

"*What?!*" Crom complains. "No! What about you?"

"I'll hold them off as long as I can," he says. "I've lived a lot of lives. Nothing they do to me could be worse than what I've already been through. If this is the end, then so be it. Just do me a favor. Tell Daizy— *Ack!*" He winces as a bolt of pain shoots through his wound.

"Ack!" Crom repeats, scribbling in her notebook. "Got it."

Ol' Garth rubs up against Adam's legs, and as the cat plods away, it says, "Mealtime is never going to be the same."

"But how are we going to find our way out of the woods without you?" D'ohry sobs.

"Na-nu will guide you," Adam says, the dirt in front of him smoking as he sprinkles it with holy water. "This is his domain."

"No way," the demon child lies. "I would never betray my own kind. These are the most powerful badargh demons in the whole forest."

The devil suddenly lets out a pained howl and presses its paws over its ears. "*What'd I tell you?*"

Wrapping their arms around their mutilated teacher, the kids give the old space pirate a goodbye hug before following Na-nu back toward the forest.

But watching them wander off lost and afraid as they step into the darkness, Adam gets an idea. "Wait a space second," he calls, a little bit of his old scrapper courage returning. "We're not just gonna let these fish heads get away with stealing my stuff, are we?"

"Well, what're we supposed to do, you noid?" Spuck asks.

Throwing another splash of holy water onto the dirt in front of him, Adam shakes his broken finger at Na-nu. "That thing you said before, what was it?"

"That I'm a good boy?" Na-nu says. "I am, you know."

"Not that," Adam growls. "The other thing, about the chitheads who are trying to take our souls."

The demon kid thinks for a long moment, and finally says, "Just that they're a couple of really bad demons."

As the last drops of holy water burn up at Adam's feet, the beast and the little devil lunge across the camp. But the moment they hear Na-nu's lies, they suddenly crumple to the ground.

"That's it!" Adam says. "Their weakness is flattery. Everybody, lay it on thick."

Stepping toward the fire, Crom announces, "You two are so strong, do you work out?"

"No!" the devil screams.

"And they're smart," Spuck says. "Like, they managed to trick all of us without even trying."

Gnashing at the ether, the beast says, "I'm going to eat your souls."

"But you're just so cute!" When D'ohry pinches the red devil's cheek, her fingers singe its flesh.

With an unholy screech, the devil cries, "Let's get the fraiche out of here!"

The beast digs its hooves in as the little ackle bounces off into the dark. But when the smiling kids approach with their arms outstretched to administer a deadly group hug, the big demon turns tail and clumsily stomps after its evil companion.

Once Adam is convinced that they're really, truly not coming back, he collapses onto his tapes. "I can't believe that actually worked."

"I guess that's why they call him Asteroid Jones," Ham says, laying his flickering body onto the dirt.

"So, what do we do now?" D'ohry asks, her hair a rainbow fluff ball as she plops down in front of the fire.

"Maybe watching another one of Mr. Jones's deaths will lift our spirits," Crom suggests.

"Good idea," Adam says, but as he searches for the next tape, he notices a dark shadow slinking past the fire. "Hey, where do you think you're going?"

Glancing back at them, its lips stretched in a predatory grin too big for its cute little head, Ol' Garth says, "It's hunting season, and I'm hunting demons."

# 76

"I left some rations out for you in the kitchen," Grandpa says as he slips into his solar windbreaker. "And remember to listen for the atmospheric genny." He points at the digital gauge on the wall which indicates that the current oxygen level inside the dome is safely within the yellow 'warning' zone. "It's been acting up lately, so if it goes out, you'll have to run out back and get it started again." Holding his finger up, he says, "Listen… Can you hear it?"

"Of course I can hear it," I tell him. "I've been able to hear it every space second of every space day since I got here. I'll be fine. Now, go have fun with your friends."

A deafening *BRROOONK* rattles the house, and Grandpa shouts, *"That must be B_req. I'll seeya later."*

I jut my thumb at him as he heads out the front door, and suddenly, for the first time in my pre-adult life, I'm home alone. As the ringing in my ears fades, a flurry of incoherent possibilities bounce around my adolescent brain, the first being, of course, to finally check out the adult video selection. But something about porn made by people who have been dead for hundreds of years suddenly feels somehow off-putting. So, I decide to watch Grandpa's latest pick instead.

Stripping down to my boxers, I scurry to the den to pop the tape in, and as it's starting, I head to the kitchen to pick out a ration. The old man left me three varieties – Moon Cheez Pizza, Clone Meat Nuggets with Moon Tubers, and Mystery Dinner. I spend a few space minutes contemplating my choices before it occurs to me that tonight I don't have to choose. Instead, I rip all three packages open, stuff them into the oven, and crank the heat.

While I wait for my dinners to cook, I set out in search of a beverage worthy of accompanying a feast of so many portions. The occasion calls for something a little more sophisticated than recycled tap water. So, I hunt through the fridge for a flat soda or a forgotten carton of chocolate multi-milk. But I come out empty-handed.

"I guess it's TW for me," I announce to no one.

But as I begin to shut the refrigerator door, something – call it intuition, Space God, or the will of the universe itself – urges me to check the crisper, and I slide it open to find a dozen glistening gold cans of Ol' Guard.

When my rations are ready, I arrange my meal on a TV tray in the den before plopping into Grandpa's tattered recliner and cracking one of the six cold ones I set out for myself. I take my first sip, allowing the subtle belchy flavor to wash over my tongue as I tour the grounds of Faber College. Unlike my first beer, this one goes down smooth.

The next thing I know, I'm waking to a blank screen and a pounding head. Empty ration trays and beer cans tumble off me as I sit up. I have no idea how long I've been out, but Grandpa apparently hasn't gotten back yet. Except for the ringing in my ears, the house is quiet.

I switch the TV over to Misery Acres News, but something feels off, so I mute it. *"Grandpa?"*

There's no answer, and in fact, no sound at all, not even... That's when it hits me. Shoving the TV tray over, I try to stand, but I'm too weak, so I slide onto the floor and crawl across the den on my hands and knees. By the time I reach the hallway, I feel like I'm going to pass out. I take a few deep breaths as I pull my body toward the kitchen, and propping my back inside the doorway, I manage to push myself onto my feet. With my head spinning and vision blurring, I spot the blinking red light confirming my doom, and all I can do is laugh.

"I suffocated before I hit the floor," Adam says as the colorless flames flicker over the campsite. "That fishing generator..."

Looking up from her notebook, Crom tells him, "That's horrific."

"No chit."

"What ever happened to this Grandpa guy?" she asks.

The old scrapper gazes out into the rustling ghost wood, as if the answer lay somewhere in the petrified shadows. "Your angelic teacher, BM, claims the old man isn't here. But that's all I can get out of the holy ackle."

"There's one thing I don't get," Ham says, his flickering jaw resting on his knees. "What the fraiche is Faber College?"

"You mean BM hasn't even taught you the ABCs of comedy?" Adam moans, glancing at the blank faces huddled around the fire. "*Animal House*, *Blues Brothers*, *Caddyshack* – learn them. Live them."

Shaking in her neon sneakers as the pained howls of a suffering demon echo through the trees, D'ohry asks, "So, what now?"

"We get the fish out of here," Adam tells them, the bite marks surrounding his shoulder having nearly healed. As they prepare to step back out into the dark, he hastily collects the tapes strewn around the fire and gets to work reorganizing them in chronological order.

"Can't you just stuff them back in your bag?" Spuck asks, plucking a stray strand of demon spittle off his tux t-shirt.

Adam slowly turns his head to glare at the young soul, and Spuck backs off. It doesn't take long for the old scrapper to get his memories back in order, but as he starts slipping them into their carrier, something is amiss. He's not sure what it is, but his 'tape sense' is tingling. Taking inventory of his collection, he counts and then recounts and then re-recounts them. But he keeps coming up short.

"What is it?" Crom asks.

"Rat farts!" Adam says, counting them again. "I'm missing four tapes."

"Are you sure?"

"Of course I'm sure!" he snaps. "Daizy has one, so that means those demons still have the other three. Either that, or they're hidden around here somewhere." Head spinning, he frantically searches the campsite, tossing aside demonic stuffed animals and cursed souvenirs. But the tapes are nowhere to be found. "Everybody calm down. We'll just wait here for the demons to come back and force them, under threat of flattery, to give me back my memories."

The kids glance at each other skeptically as Crom approaches the old scrapper and gently lays her hand on his shoulder. "I don't think they're coming back."

Looking into his bag at the missing pieces of his life, Adam whimpers, "But I already forget which ones they were."

"All right, old man," Spuck says, padding through the dirt in his sandals. "Enough is enough. So, you're missing a few short moments of some past life. We're missing this one right now."

"Maybe *you* took them." The old scrapper snatches his bag and presses it to his chest as he backs away from the kids. "That's what this is all about, isn't it? This whole time you were just after my tapes. Well, I'm onto you!"

"That's ridiculous!" Spuck cries, and groaning, he grabs onto Adam's bony arm. "We'll drag you out of here if we have to."

As they struggle in the gray firelight, a soft whine gradually rises over their bickering, soon growing into an earsplitting wail that forces the whole camp to its knees.

Once Na-nu has their attention, the young demon quits howling and tells them, "Since you all asked, I don't know where the tapes are either. I certainly didn't trade them to pay off any staggering debts to any all-powerful demons who were threatening to torture me for the rest of eternity, if that's what you're implying."

As Adam translates the backward words, he cries, "You pawned my memories!"

"I don't know what you're talking about," the evil kid says, dodging a plush cacodemon as he scurries around the fire. "And I definitely can't show you exactly where they are."

Ceasing his toy attack, Adam says, "That means you *will* show us, right?"

"No," Na-nu tells him.

"O-kay…"

"No means yes," Crom says.

"Right, so he's gonna take us to the tapes," Adam declares, glaring at the little suspendered demon. "But I wonder, can we trust him?"

Seeming to think the question over, Na-nu finally shakes his head and says, "No."

**77**

When I'm done tightening the final bolt to secure the charred captain's chair we scrapped from the *Asteroid Jones*, I plunk down in the open cockpit and gaze up at the stars. I can hardly wait to get out there.

As I slug down the rest of the beer I copped from Grandpa's stash, I look over the plans he drew up for us – not dissimilar to his designs for the original junker, but with a few modifications. Most of it is indecipherable, but I figure I should at least be able to install the fridge magnets without too much trouble. But I'm going to need another drink.

Climbing back down into the yard, I toss my empty can deep in the scrap where Grandpa won't find it, and I head back to the house. Per usual, the TV at the end of the hall is blaring as I sneak through the front door and into the kitchen. Whatever he's watching sounds awful, but when I open the fridge, I discover something even worse – there's only one beer left.

I've been careful about my theft thus far, sneaking out two or three cans per case without him noticing, but I can't imagine a universe in which he wouldn't miss his last cold one. No matter how I look at it, I fail to conceive of a way to take the beer without getting caught. But then I remember the old scrapper motto – drink now, worry later.

So, I crack the can, and as I raise it to my lips, I hear something crash in the other room. After a brief moment of drunken hesitation, I run down the hall and into the den, where I find Grandpa lying facedown in a pool of his own ration.

"Don't do this to me," I warn him as I flip his motionless body over. "You're the only one I have left."

But as I lean down to check if he's breathing, he suddenly lunges forward and wraps his arms around me.

*"Ughh,"* he moans, a thick glob of gray ration mush hanging off his chin.

*"This isn't happening,"* I mutter as I use all my power to wrest myself free from the zombie's grasp, but his old man strength is impossible to overcome.

"Tha-," he croaks, as if trying to tell me something. "That's… *MY BEER!*"

*"Pfft*, yeah right," Spuck says, ambling through the dark forest in his flip-flops. "That was like one of those movies you're always talking about."

"Grandpa wasn't a real zombie," Adam clarifies. "He was just trying to scare me out of drinking his beer. And it worked, for a while."

As they follow Na-nu deeper into the ghost wood, Cromula tells Adam, "This place gives me the creeps. There's ghosts everywhere, and I keep getting the feeling that we're being followed. Are you sure we can trust this little liar? What if he's leading us to some crazy powerful demon that's going to eat our souls?"

"He might do that," Adam concedes, flinching at the sound of a nearby moan. "But right now he's our best hope and the only one of us who knows these woods. You want to finish your map, don't you?"

"Well…" She pulls her green ponytail tight as she considers. "Yes."

"Hey, I think I see something," Ham announces, his flickering aura just visible in the darkness up ahead.

Sure enough, Adam can make out a dark glow in the distance, and as the demon kid leads them closer, a great shadow looms up out of the ghost wood. A dark castle shrouded in shadow, black light flickers from torches lining the palace's crooked walls as tortured howls cry out from within, all of which gets Adam to thinking that maybe this wasn't such a good idea after all.

Marching out ahead, Crom taps her finger against the side of the evil structure and announces, "Ghost brick - strong stuff. They must be hiding something valuable."

"There has to be another way," Adam decides. "Maybe we could find a demon back at the bar who will accept a painful pooping memory to retrieve the tape for us. I can afford to sacrifice one of those."

But before they can decide how to proceed, Na-nu is already knocking on the enormous petrified door. The old space pirate tries to drag the kid away from the stoop, but soon the door creaks open. The demon that answers is a lumbering creature with gray skin and a vacant stare who looks as undead as the surrounding trees.

"*Huhhh?*" the monster groans, its bathrobe hanging open to reveal a soiled white undershirt and checked boxer shorts.

"Uh, we're here to rent," Na-nu says.

"*Mmm…*" The monster nods its thick head and turns to stomp back into the castle.

"Should we go in?" Crom asks.

After some deep thought, Adam finally shrugs. "I guess so."

Sticking close together, they follow the monster down dark corridors and up treacherous stairs made of polished ghost wood rubbed smooth from countless eons of hoof traffic, until they arrive at a cavernous chamber deep inside the castle. The room is dim, its contents obscured. Black flames crackle inside a large ghost brick fireplace, the dark light providing them with only the vaguest sense of their surroundings.

"*Wuhhh…*" their monstrous host moans, leaving them on their own as it shuffles off into the shadows.

Warming his hands by the fire, Adam says, "I guess that means wait." He can't explain it, but he can sense a sick energy emanating from this place. Even more worrying, he doesn't entirely hate it.

"Back so soon?" a soft, devilish voice calls out from the darkness. "And you brought friends. Your capacity for self-punishment knows no bounds."

As the slinky demon steps into the dark light of the fire, Adam can feel her probing the worst parts of his mind. Using some sort of black magic, she raises her finger, and his head slowly lifts until he's staring into her fiery eyes. Her crimson skin is so tempting that he reaches out to touch it, and she smacks his hand away.

"Trust me, you wouldn't survive," she says, stroking his chin. "Looks like Na-nu brought me some new customers. That's one way to pay me off. So, what do you want?"

When she breaks eye contact, her spell lifts, and Adam regains enough control of his divine urges to tell her, "I want my memory tape back."

Looking him up and down, her blood red lips twisting, she says, "I recognize you. You're that scrapper, with the beer. I've enjoyed your suffering."

"Yeah, well, you said it – it's *my* suffering, and I want it back."

"Silly boy." Leaning in close, she gently whispers into his ear, "Your suffering belongs to me."

While Adam is in his weakened state, the monster that led them through the castle gradually stomps out of the shadows and latches onto the scrapper's arms, moaning, *"Ughhh…"*

"There's no point in struggling," the demon says. "Slog is one of the strongest monsters in all of Other Side. Now if I could just teach him to shut the *fraiching door…"*

"What do you think you're doing?" Crom shouts. "That may just look like some old lost soul who can't keep track of his memories, but that's Asteroid Jones you're messing with!"

"You hear that, Slog?" the evil woman says. "We caught us a celebrity. Although, I find it hard to believe that this shriveled spirit is the famous space pirate."

"Well, believe it," the girl says as the kids ineffectively pummel the house monster. "I knew we shouldn't have trusted that little liar."

Slithering up beside the helpless scrapper, the nubs of her horns poking out from underneath her dark bangs, the demon tells Adam, "Let's get one thing straight. I rent. I don't sell. Na-nu should have told you that, though I know it can be difficult to understand what the fraiche the little arghole is saying. In any case, that memory was payment for the considerable debt he accrued browsing my collection."

"But he stole it from *me*," Adam argues. "It wasn't his to sell."

"What's the old scrapper saying?" she asks him. "Finders keepers?" Leaning in close, she flicks her tongue over his neck. "That tape is a valuable piece of merchandise. However, I'm always open to interesting trades. I know you're holding out on me. I can sense your pain."

Abandoning her flashy yet pointless assault on Adam's thick-headed captor, D'ohry looks up and says, "Save some for later, lady, fraiche."

Adam briefly imagines what it would be like to have the demon's hairy thighs wrapped around his neck, but when he comes to, he questions, "Rentals? Collection? What the fish is this place, anyway?"

"I'll make you a deal," she tells him as she grinds up against his soul. "I'll show you mine if you show me yours."

# 78

The virtual classroom is overly crowded today, packed with rowdy avatars searching for last chance credit before the final. Somebody must have gained access to the room's settings because our location keeps changing — one space second we're sitting inside one of the great chain coffee shops of ancient Earth, and the next we're in a crude reproduction of Springfield Elementary. Most of the other students don't seem bothered by the shifting scenery, but it's giving me digital sickness.

Even though I plugged in late, the teacher still isn't here, so I take the opportunity to download some more useless information about the 73rd Annual Robot Uprising into my brain.

"They should just call it 'The One With the Ration Shortage,'" somebody says, and I pause the download to find a spikey-haired cyber girl with big animated eyes sitting at the desk in front of me.

She seems to be waiting for me to say something, so I blurt, "Uh, yeah…"

Smiling nervously, she says, "I have to tell you something."

"Uh, yeah?"

"I think you forgot something."

"Huh?" I ask, mesmerized by her programmed beauty.

She points down, and I look at the bottom half of my digitized body to discover nothing but two bare legs and a black censor bar.

Covering my shame, I cry, "Oh Space God, is this a nightmare?"

"Nope," the girl says, holding back laughter. "This is real virtual life."

Fumbling open my character settings, I equip the first pants I lay eyes on, a pair of tight pink leggings designed for an avatar with a much different design, and I brace myself for ridicule. But as I glance around the simulated classroom at the purple *T. rex* in neon board shorts and the perpetually melting boy feverishly trying to multi-down an entire semester's worth of information, I realize that none of the other kids are paying any attention to me.

Giggling at my humiliation, the cyber girl leans across my desk and whispers in my ear, "You're cute."

As she turns back around, I vaguely notice the teacher materialize at the front of the class. He must have accidentally set his avatar to display his actual appearance, because it looks like chit.

The loud chatter ends abruptly when he mutes the room, and holding onto his forehead, he says, "If you haven't already heard, your previous, *hic,* teacher is no longer employed at this virtual learning, *hic,* institution. She wasn't even here for a whole space year before the United, *hic,* Empires plucked her away to the Promised

Land. But what about Mr. Klud? When does he get a, *hic*, fancy onworld condo with a natural atmosphere and working holo-tube and those, *hic*, little umbrellas that keep the moon dust out of your, *hic*, drinks…" Once it becomes clear that none of us have the answers, he sends out the test and mutes himself to silently weep at his desk.

I know I know the answers, but as the rest of the class gets to work, all I can do is stare at the back of the cyber girl's head, imagining the rest of our life together. Somehow I manage to fill in the blanks, and when the test is over, I get insta-graded with a smirking emoji.

When I look up, the girl is laughing at me, big tear icons flowing from her cartoon eyes. The room being muted, she points to the top of my head, and after a few space seconds of confusion, I make my username visible – *asteroidjones*.

For a moment, she pretends like she's not going to give me hers, but soon the name *Jexxy_Silverstar* appears above her spiky head. She mouths something to me, and as she logs off, the word lingers in the air in a virtual puff of artificial cherry smoke – '*Ciao*.'

"So what," the curvy demon scoffs. "It was death at first sight?"

"Yep," Adam says, sighing wearily at the ancient memory as he slips it back in his bag. "Either that or the clogged air filter filling grandpa's house with toxic exhaust."

"I must admit, I was hoping for something a little less pleasant," she says, clomping toward him and yanking his hair back. "But I can tell you are a collector after my own black heart. You understand the value of a death, unlike most of the lost souls haunting these woods. So, I'm going to let you experience all the horrors I have to offer. Just be careful – they can be addicting. But you already know that."

She snaps her fingers, and dark torches blaze to life along the walls, revealing floor-to-ceiling ghost wood shelves stacked with memory objects. Adam recognizes a few of the items from his lives, including a grimy Earthball cap and a little rubber vending machine *yōkai*. But the most interesting thing about the collection is how unremarkable it is, full of the kind of incidental ephemera happened upon and usually quickly forgotten and discarded throughout the course of a life.

"Well, what do you think?" the demon asks, apparently waiting for Adam's appraisal.

"Uh, it's…" he says, trailing off. "What is it?"

"You disappoint me, space pirate." As she turns to pace the room, Adam notices two gory knobs protruding from her shoulders where her divine appendages were gracelessly hacked off. "Like your videotapes, every object on these shelves holds the eternal record of a living spirit experiencing a moment of intense suffering. Considering the quantity and fetishistic organization of the tapes in that bag of yours, I thought that you of all souls would appreciate such a collection."

Careful not to fall under a logic spell, Adam says, "But it's not the suffering I enjoy. I like to revisit my own deaths as a reminder of what it's like to be *alive*, and I like to keep them organized because *how else would you keep them?*"

"You want to know what I think?" the demon asks.

"No."

"I think you're just like the rest of these lost souls, except where their only option is to sacrifice what little remains of their eternal souls for a quick fix, you've got a permanent supply."

"And what the fish are you?" Adam demands. "*Who* are you, anyway?"

"I'm merely a collector and facilitator, not a user," the demon says. "I take great pains in tracking down the choicest, most agonizing memory objects, and I provide an invaluable service lending them to those who would come looking. I must sample the goods from time to time to confirm their authenticity, of course, but I'm largely immune to the long term effects. As to precisely *who* I am, it would take the better part of a lifetime to pronounce one syllable of my true—"

"Yeah, all right," Adam cuts her off. "Well, we've blown a lot of time here already, so if you could just get me my tape, we can extricate ourselves from this whole... *thing* you've got going on here."

Scrunching her perfect evil nose, she argues, "But time is only relevant in-universe."

"Nevertheless..."

"In any case, I'm afraid I can't do that." She stares into his eyes, and he feels himself weakening under her sexy influence. "Your tapes are an integral part of my collection now. They're going to help usher in a new era of cruelty. Demons, and angels, will come from all over Other Side to witness the deaths of Asteroid Jones, and before long the entire realm will be in hock to me!"

Sensing that the conversation is about to take a problematic turn, Adam clutches his bag as tight as his old fingers will clutch and says, "I can't help but notice you said 'deaths.'"

"Don't worry," she tells him. "You can rent them anytime you want."

"Nah, I think I'll hold onto them," he says as the house monster grabs the strap of his bag.

"Oh, for fraiche sake!" Cromula cries, rolling up her travel uniform in an attempt to rally the rest of the cowering kids. "We have to do something. Can't one of you manifest some holy powder or water or *something* to save us?"

"You know we've all been having trouble manifesting," D'ohry says, pointing to her stained sneakers. "But maybe if I keep it simple." Holding her arm out, the sparkly aura surrounding her hand gradually intensifies, until the room is flooded with white light.

The flare only lasts a moment, but after it goes out, the demon and her monster are left howling and stumbling around the room.

"I want those tapes!" she screams, blindly clawing at the ether.

"We have to hurry," D'ohry says. "I don't have the energy to do that again."

Adam frantically glances between the various shadowy passageways leading out of the dim room and cries, "*Which way do we go?*"

"This way," Crom says, pointing to a dark doorway surrounded by shelves full of used napkins and overused nudie magazines.

With the help of her map, they pile out into the dark corridor and back down the slippery staircase. Adam begins to think they might even make it out of the castle alive, but somehow they veer off course, and as they try to find their way back to the front door, they wind up even more lost.

"There's something wrong with the map," Crom says. "It's not working right."

"What are we going to do?!" D'ohry cries, her sneakers flashing in the dark.

As Adam's eyes adjust to the dark, he's suddenly able to make out a long hallway lined with irregular doors, and he suggests, "Let's try one of these rooms. Maybe we'll find a sympathetic monster or something that will help us escape." Feeling along the wall, he grabs onto the first handle he can find and yanks the door open.

# 360

"It's another cloudless morning," I report into my audio recorder as I traipse through the colorful underbrush. "Although the thick rainbow canopy has been effective in shielding me from direct exposure to the suns, I can nevertheless feel myself baking in my travel britches. The humidity has been so bad that I can scarcely remember what dry is.

"The jungle is suffocating. The brush grows almost as fast as I can slice through it with my knife saber. The blanket of new growth wrapped around me when I awoke this morning was particularly unnerving. There was a moment that I thought about allowing myself to be swallowed up like so much plant food. But I've got too much riding on this expedition. The fate of the galaxy's arcades hangs in the balance.

"Unfortunately, I have yet to discover any trace of my elusive prey. I'm loath to admit it, but it's possible the old boys back home were right. Maybe the sightings *can* be attributed to misidentified space junk, and all the explorers who disappeared just got lost wandering the jungle. But for birthdays' sake, I hope they're wrong."

Sliding the recorder back into my pocket, I unclip my canteen and endure a long swig of hot rainwater before continuing on. It's not long before I come upon a thick vine blocking my path, but when I move to dispatch it, my foot slips in something soft and I crash to the forest floor. As soon as I come to, I yank my boot off to give it a scraping, only to discover that the dung caked inside the treads is no ordinary chit.

Pale turquoise, with the consistency of chunky cookie dough, I hold it up to my nose and administer the sniff test. "Jellybeans."

When I hear a cute giggle emerge from the bushes nearby, I quickly stuff my foot back in my boot and jump to my feet. Stepping cautiously through the brush, I come out into a small clearing, where I spot the most incredible creature I've ever seen.

It's a tiny thing, covered in blue fur and waddling around on stunted legs. With its big glassy eyes and oversized smile, it looks just like any other stuffed animal behind the prize counter, only better. I figure it'll bring in a thousand tickets, easy.

I smile at the little plush monster, raising my knife as I move in for the kill. But when I get close, the creature suddenly notices me, and for a split space second I see the flash of its fangs as they sink into my leg.

The knife flies from my hand, and I frantically circle the clearing with the squishy animal hanging off me, its jaws refusing to unclamp. Although I know it's pointless, I yelp for help, and to my surprise, help arrives. Only, it's not for me.

The monsters grin madly as they step out of the trees, their glassy eyes staring into my soul as their giant, fingerless limbs muffle my screams.

I'm groggy when I wake, and feeling something in my mouth, I spit out a big wad of stuffing. As my senses return, I realize that I'm high up off the ground, surrounded by a gang of giant spastic aliens.

"Gimme the ugly one for starters," somebody says, and I glance out past the abyss between me and the prize counter to see a living stuffed animal of ill-proportion handing over an armful of tickets. "I promised I'd get my little sister something to chew on."

As I'm passed from one grinning monster to the next, I find myself heading toward the horrid jaws of the teething toddler with a full accounting of my worth – precisely seventy-five tickets.

When the memory ends, the door opens, and Adam is crushed underneath a pile of kids tumbling back out into the hallway.

"I'll never look at a stuffed animal the same way again," D'ohry says, her hair a big rainbow puffball as she stares off into the ether.

With his sunglasses askew but his cool otherwise intact, Spuck asks, "What the fraiche was that?"

"It wasn't one of *my* deaths," the old scrapper says, barely able to pick himself up off the floor. "It must be part of the demon's collection. We have to find somewhere less traumatizing to hide before she finds us and adds the rest of my tapes to her museum of suffering." Grabbing the handle of the nearest door, he wrenches it open and finds himself in the middle of a fireworks factory just as some scrambled egghead is about to light a cigarette. After he pulls himself back together, he shuts the door and announces, "That's not gonna work."

"Come on," Spuck tells Ham, patting his pixelated pal on the back. "*We'll* get us out of here!" The two of them disappear inside one of the rooms, and a few moments later they're violently expelled in a torrent of green slime.

"Well?" Adam says, standing over the crumpled spirits. "What was in there?"

As the ooze covering them fades into the ether, the boys glance at each other and simultaneously moan, "I don't want to talk about it."

"What are we going to do now?" D'ohry whimpers, balled up on the carpet.

"Don't worry, you guys." Flashing the others the Pants symbol, Cromula whips her green ponytail and looks to their teacher for guidance. "Asteroid Jones will get us out of this."

Adam tries to think of what the old space pirate in him would do, but he can't remember. All he knows is that if he doesn't act fast, they might all become permanent exhibits. "Maybe if I just…" Bracing himself, he cracks one of the doors and peeks inside to find an empty hallway. "This could be our way out!"

As he steps inside, the hall grows so dark that he can no longer see the outlines of the other doors around him. It soon becomes apparent that there's something strange about this part of the house. The ether smells sour and rotten, and the carpet feels different, the way it squishes under his feet. Emboldened by the sounds of the ghost wood up ahead, he holds his hands out, blindly feeling his way forward until he senses the space open up around him. For a brief moment, he's relieved to be outside again, but as the ghostly moaning gets louder, he starts to feel a growing unease deep in his gut.

Trudging through the sludge as fast as he can lift his soggy boat shoes, he suddenly senses that he's not alone. His hand shakes as he reaches into his pocket for the lighter he bought especially for this vacation. But when he tries to ignite it, the goop from his fingers keeps it from sparking. Wiping the lighter on his moist floral shirt, he gives it a few more flicks, and it flares to life. Only, he almost wishes it hadn't.

A fatalistic laugh escapes his lips as he gazes out across the pool of bile at the moaning half dead, clad in their straw hats and clutching their colorful drinks as the creature's stomach acid gradually dissolves their artificially toned bodies. Before long, the flame flickers out, and although it wasn't mentioned in the brochure, he's treated to a slow, painful death.

When Adam finally crawls back out into the hallway, he tells the kids, "We gotta get the fish out of here."

"*Could we?*" Spuck pleads.

"Butt up, you guys," Crom says. "Do you hear that?"

Somewhere off in the shadows, not far from where they're cowering, Adam can make out the distinct sound of the demon's monster servant lumbering in their direction. Thinking slow, he leads the kids further down the hall, and they soon come to a dead end.

As the monster's footsteps stomp closer, he says, "We're going to have to try another one of these doors."

"But we're just going to get killed again!" D'ohry argues.

"We can either face the horrors in there, or we can take our chances with the monsters out here. Besides, it's a good character builder," he tells them, and pulling the door open, they stumble into the darkness.

A new type of silence takes hold as Adam readies himself for a painful mauling, or vaporization, or banana peel. But it never comes.

"Wh-where are we?" Crom finally asks.

Lifting his head, the old space pirate is startled to discover what feels like a bunch of monster skins hanging from the ceiling, when it dawns on him. "I think it's a closet."

79

The room is so dark that for a moment I can't remember where I am. But when I reach down into the couch cushions for whatever is digging into my spine, I find an object that brings me crashing back to reality. Cracking the tab, I lift the can high to toast the space gods, when the lights flick on.

"Aha," I laugh nervously, the warm one raised to my lips.

"Never drink and fly," the old man scolds as he stomps across the cabin and snatches the beer from my hand. Downing it in a few big gulps, he throws the empty can to the floor and belches, "*BUAAA…*"

"Wait, you mean…"

"Just finished calibrating the engine," Grandpa says. "She's all yours."

"I can't believe it's really happening!" He tosses me the keys, but they slip through my fingers, and I reverentially scramble to retrieve them off the floor. "I can finally get off of this chithole rock. No offense."

"Well, some taken," Grandpa says. "But come on out and take a look at her first. I think you're gonna like the paint job, or my name isn't Silas Ichabod Jones."

Climbing down through the cargo hold, we step out into the yard, and I look up to find the old words sloppily scrawled across the junker's hull.

"That's really great," I tell him. "But I think I can make it even better." Grabbing his paint can, I climb up the ladder leaning against the ship and add two vertical lines after the 's' in *Asteroid Jones*. "There."

Grandpa smiles up at me, his eyes welling with tears. "I love it. Now, go make her purr."

For the first time in a long time, as I take my seat in the thirdhand captain's chair, I feel alive. Even though I had to get Grandpa to co-sign the loan, and I owe more credits than I care to calculate on the engine and all the other parts we couldn't salvage from the yard, I figure it should only take a few short space years of hard scrapping before she's all paid off.

As I slip the key into the slot on the dash, I say the old scrapper's prayer, "Bless this mess," and by some miracle, the engine hums to life. Leaning across the passenger seat, I yell to Grandpa, *"I'm gonna take her up!"*

*"Okay, but be careful,"* he shouts back. *"The controls are a little tricky."*

*"Pfft,"* I scoff as I seal up the window. "I beat the final boss in the simulator. I think I know what I'm doing." Once she's pressurized, I take hold of the spatial orienter, and we lift off into the infinite unknown.

"Do you really think this is the best time to be learning about your deaths?" Spuck whispers from the back of the demon's coat closet. "We're about to find out what it's like firsthand."

"Would you butt up?" Crom growls, her penlight wagging furiously as she updates her journal. "I want to find out what happened."

Shoving aside a bloody rain slicker, Adam says, "Just because we're in immortal danger doesn't mean you get to skip out on your schoolwork. Anyway, the ship crashed because *somebody* forgot to charge the fuel cells."

"Who?" Crom asks.

"Uh, I can't remember…"

Leaning her bright head against the door, D'ohry closes her eyes and whimpers, "We're going to be stuck in here watching these crummy videos for eternity, aren't we?"

"Nah," Adam consoles her. "I've been in worse scraps than this. We'll be out of here in half an eternity, tops." When something crinkles behind him, he flinches and spins around. "What was that?" Grabbing Crom's pen, he shines the light along the back of the closet and finds Ham stuffing a handful of irregular Morlock rinds into his angel face.

"I'm sorry," the boy says. "I snack when I'm scared."

"Gimme those." Adam snatches the bag from Ham's fist and munches one of the stale rinds. "*Hmph*, not bad."

"*Shhh*," Crom says. "Somebody's coming."

The old space pirate presses his ear against the door and listens as the monster slowly shambles toward their hiding spot. The big flunky stops just outside the closet and releases a confused grunt before angrily stomping around the empty corridor, wailing and pounding on the walls. The top half of the door suddenly splinters apart as the monster smashes its fist through the wooden blinds, and the class fearfully retreats behind the gory outerwear.

"I thought you said you heard something down here," the demon's satiny voice complains from the hallway.

"*Guh*," Slog responds.

"Well, I don't see anything," she says. "We can't let them escape. You're sure you locked the front door?"

"Yuh…"

There's a long skeptical pause, and she finally says, "Let's check the library again. I know that scrapper's type. He won't leave without his precious tape."

As they shuffle away, Adam cautiously cracks what's left of the closet door and waves for the others to follow. "Come on. This is our chance."

Keeping a good distance, the class creeps after the demon and her house monster, winding through the dark hallways back toward the front of the castle.

"I get it now," Crom says as she traces their route. "The ghost brick must be causing the map to invert. I'll make a note in the legend."

Once they have their bearings, they abandon their evil guides in favor of a series of familiar passageways leading them back to the castle entrance, where they find the door wide open. All they have to do is walk out. But as the kids laugh and skip toward the dark forest, Adam gets a nagging reminder that his bag is still light.

When Crom looks back and sees he isn't following them, she asks, "What's wrong?"

"It's nothing," he tells her. "Go on ahead. I'll be right behind you. Here, take these." He tosses her the rest of his tapes, and before she can argue, he shuffles back into the castle.

This time, he carefully traces and retraces his steps as he scrambles through the halls and up the slippery staircase, until he finds his way back to the dark library. Detecting no sign of the demon or her monster, he tiptoes into the dim room and frantically searches the collection of death baubles.

When he spots his lost memory precariously displayed on a shelf above the fireplace, he climbs onto the adjacent unit and reaches out over the dark flames. Barely able to brush its case with the tips of his fingers, he accidentally knocks the tape off the shelf. He instinctively thrusts his hand toward the flames, and by some miracle manages to snatch the fragile memory before it can fall into the fire.

A wave of relief washes over him as he descends the display case, his tape unharmed and in hand. But the feeling is soon replaced by regret as he slips on the remains of someone's old virtual pet, bringing the whole unit crashing down on top of him.

By the time he manages to unbury himself, the demon is standing over him with her monster in tow and fury in her eyes. Squeezing the tape to his chest, Adam braces his soul for a violent rending. But when they fail to tear into him, he looks up to find them backing away, their faces twisted in revulsion.

"Now you've done it!" the demon howls.

"*Gah!*" the monster moans, cowering behind its bathrobe.

"What are you talking ab—" Adam starts to ask, but then he sees it, hovering near the flames. "Oh…"

Smiling its dumb smile as it drifts through the room, the lost soul says, "Now you're really not going to make it."

"Once you have ghosts, you can never get rid of them," the demon cries, thrashing her monster. "I told you to *shut the door*!"

"How did it find me?" Adam asks.

The demon's skin smokes as she turns her rage toward the crumpled scrapper. "You mean it was you who brought that disgusting thing in here?" Stomping across the room, she pulls Adam up by his bootleg *Horror Workout* t-shirt and whispers, "I want you and that pest out of here."

"My pleasure," he says, but as he limps for the door, she rips the tape out of his hand. "*Aww…*"

"I'll let you leave with your soul, if only to keep that ghost from attaching itself to my castle," she says. "But the tape belongs to me."

"Told you," the ghost tells him.

"Chut up, you!" he says, swatting at the hazy spirit.

Finding himself backed into a dark corner, Adam is left with no choice but to do the one thing he was so desperately trying to avoid.

# 80

The stars twinkle different on the other side of the dome. They're the same ones that surround me at all space hours, but somehow they seem brighter out here. Maybe I've just never really looked.

Gazing into the fundamental fabric of reality, I get the sensation that I'm drowning and flying at the same time. I've lived my whole life in the universe, but I never noticed how big it really is. It's, like, the biggest thing I've ever seen, by a long shot. Just thinking about it makes me parched.

Feeling around the dark cabin, I locate my beer and guzzle what's left of it before tossing the crumpled can to the floor and grabbing another flat one from the box under the dash. It took me more than a space year, but I finally managed to swipe a whole case worth, one can at a time, under Grandpa's inebriated watch. It required more self-restraint than I knew I possessed not to drink them ahead of time, but it was worth it to properly commemorate the maiden voyage of the *Asteroid Jones II*.

It's hard to believe I'm finally the captain of my own ship. I keep thinking I'm going to wake up and realize it was all just a drunk dream. But until then, I crack my second beer as a free spaceman and offer up a silent toast to the stars.

Leaning my chair back as far as it will go, I turn the engine off and get starry-eyed drifting through a secluded corner of Misery Acres as fantasies of alien worlds and space adventures flit through my head. I don't even miss TV, much.

It's unclear how long I'm daydreaming, but when I finally snap out of it, I reach for another beer and discover, to my horror, that the box is empty. I don't even remember drinking all of them. But I do feel plastered.

As I search for my phone to check the time, I remember I left it at the house so the old man couldn't bother me. It must have been space hours ago that I told him I was going for a cruise before dinner. My head spins as I search for the keys amongst the dark pile of empty beer cans surrounding the dash. Despite my best efforts, they're nowhere to be found, and as I shut my eyes to stem the tide of sick rising in my stomach, I laugh and mutter to myself, "Rat farts"

Marching through a thick bog of smelly black goop, the origins of which Adam decides he'd rather not speculate on, he says, "You know how sometimes you drop something and can't find it no matter how hard you look? Well, I guess you don't, but it's a suspiciously regular occurrence in-universe. It's gotta be some sort of design flaw. I ripped apart the whole cabin looking for those keys…"

"What the fraiche is that supposed to teach us?" Spuck asks as he fishes his sandals out of the ankle-deep muck. "The only reason you died is because you made a bunch of dumb mistakes."

"And now you have the benefit of learning from those mistakes," Adam lectures. "Don't do as I do. Do as I don't do, or something. Also, always carry a heavy key ring."

Looking up from her notebook, Crom says, "I understand from my research that spaceships from that era were usually equipped with some sort of emergency beacon. Couldn't you have sent out a rescue signal?"

"Oh yeah…," Adam says. "Well, that just further proves my point – nobody really knows what the fish they're doing."

"No spit," Spuck says.

Up ahead, Na-nu is happily skipping through the crud as he leads the dim souls either toward the rest of the tapes or their certain doom. Adam isn't sure. He's still having a space hell of a time decoding the little demon's lies.

As they march across the flatulent mud pit, the old scrapper thinks he could really use a beer. Concentrating all of his powers, he manages to manifest a dust-caked can of Ol' Guard. He stares at it skeptically for a moment, and finally raises it to his lips only to get a mouthful of thick sludge. Spitting the goop back where it came from, he hurls the can into the mud and cries, "I hate this fishing place!"

As if in reaction to his anger, a large bubble rises from the pool and releases a noxious fart cloud unlike anything Adam has ever inhaled.

"It's s-so bad…" D'ohry whimpers, sparkly tears flowing from her eyes.

"I can smell it in my soul," Ham cries, holding his ratty old t-shirt over his face. "It reminds me of the place in that movie you watched the night you lost your first tooth. I think it was called the Swamp of Asses."

Adam considers this for a moment and finally decides, "Nothing is called that!"

"It is now," Crom announces, marking the area on her map.

"*Urgh*," Adam growls, and the bog rips one.

"This might be a bad time," a wispy voice cuts in. "But I just want to remind you that you're not going to make it."

"We know!" Adam tells the annoying ghost hovering at the group's heels.

"Speaking of tapes," Crom says. "You still haven't told us how you got your death back from that demon lady."

Wringing his hands, the scrapper tells her, "I made a trade, all right? Are you happy?"

"So, what did you give her?" the nosy green-haired soul prods. "A nudie tape?"

"Let's just say it was a very *chitty* memory."

"I don't understand," she says. "Aren't all memories of equal value?"

Adam scoffs and shakes his head. "Uh… *no*."

"That's not what BM told us," D'ohry chimes.

"Eh, that angel doesn't know the first thing about chit." The old scrapper can feel his bowels growing more irritable by the moment, and as his stomach twists, he yells to Na-nu, "Where the fish are you taking us?"

The little demon takes a break from frolicking through the muck to glance back at the weary souls lagging behind him, and he points his soiled finger toward a giant mound of dark mush at the far end of the swamp.

"*Oh no…*," Adam groans. "I thought that place was just some old angel legend made up to scare young souls."

"What is it?" Crom asks. "I'll mark it on the map."

"They call it the Poop Palace."

"Buy why—" she starts only to cut herself off. "Never mind."

By the time they reach the palace gate, its excrement bars adorned with figures of famous demons cast in dried feces, the stink has grown so strong that Adam is starting to hallucinate. He almost licks what he briefly mistakes for a chocolate-covered pillar before Crom yanks him back to his senses.

It's more than a little disturbing how well Spuck and Ham are acclimating to their new surroundings, laughing carelessly as they engage in a spirited chitball fight. But when Adam notices the blank stare on D'ohry's face, he fears she may never recover.

"You guys better wait out here while I look for the tapes," Adam says. "I'll try to find them before your spirits are completely broken."

"What about you?" Crom asks.

"I'm used to being in the chit." At a glance, the fecal compound appears impenetrable, and the scrapper wonders, "But how the fish do I get inside?"

Before he can figure it out, a deep, dripping voice answers, *"Allow me..."*

A chorus of whimpers erupts behind him, and he turns to find the kids stuck in the thick puddle of chit pooling around their feet.

As the wretched waste drips up his legs, a horrid, globular face with dead eyes appears in the puddle surrounding him, and its toothless maw informs him, *"You really stepped in it now."*

# 81

Misery Acres Food and Beverage is little more than a converted moon shack attached to an old charging station, but it's the only place in the sector where I can loiter with scrappers my own age. Now that I have the *Asteroid Jones II* at my disposal, the ancient shop has become my convenience store away from home.

When I pull into the cruddy dome, a big group of belt kids is gathered outside the building, smoking space sticks and blasting scrap rock from their phones. A scraggly, bleary-eyed long hauler tells them to "turn that chit down," and they burst into a fit of laughter and profanity before cranking the music even louder. As I make my way across the dusty parking lot, the tri-clops who outbelched me in a contest the week before jokingly juts his thumb out at me, and I return the gesture.

The cramped shop is packed with a bunch of overworked, underpaid space pirates noisily gearing up for the scrapper holiday. Half of them are drinking before they even reach the counter to pay for their 80-ounce jugs of Ol' Guard and cheap Cronian moonshine. Cutting down one of the narrow snack aisles, I make my way to the back store, where they keep the expired rations and used electronics, but as usual there's not much to see.

"Aren't they ever gonna get a TV?" I wonder aloud.

"This place?" a perfectly pitched, spammy type of voice interrupts my browsing, and I look up to find a humanoid of Earth ancestry flashing me an overzealous grin. "You're not going to find anything like that in here. This is where scrap comes to die." Jutting his thumb toward the shriveled alien behind the counter, he says, "This guy's been here since the dawn of time. He wouldn't know good scrap if it landed in his backyard." It's hard to tell whether the scrapper is fifteen or fifty, but something about his unapologetic dissatisfaction with the universe at large reminds Adam of Brinx.

"I found an old UE family video player a couple space months ago," I note. "All their cartridges are censored, but still… Anyway, it's the only scrap shop in this part of the galaxy."

"Not for long!" the scrapper announces. "As soon as I collect enough inventory, I'm going to open my own shop. Some space day it'll be the biggest one in the universe."

"Good to know," I say, moving over to the bargain ration bin.

As I dig for prepackaged treasure, he tells me, "The name's Ferd, by the way. Hey, we should go scrapping together sometime. As they say, two heads are more than one."

"Yeah, maybe…" Reaching down toward the bottom of the bin, I grab one of the trays and emerge with a flavor unlike any I've ever consumed. "Holy chit, a Blue Tray Special with Moon Cheez Cake. I thought these were discontinued."

"I wouldn't eat that if I were you," Ferd advises. "It looks like it's been down there since the beginning of spacetime. You should sell it. There's a big market for vintage rations."

Clutching the dented tray, I tell him, "Nah, these things never go bad."

"O-kay," he says. "It's your space funeral."

"He was right of course," Adam tells the kids. "But you know what? That ended up being the best ration I never had. It's like, sometimes the best stuff is what kills you."

"Yeah," Spuck says, his sunglass spattered with excrement. "And sometimes it's the very expired fake food you most expect."

As D'ohry sobs in the corner of their shared latrine, Adam puts his arm around the once sparkly girl's shoulders and says, "This isn't so bad. Corporeal life is much worse. Everything is just so *real*. One space day in the universe and you'll wish you were back here in the chit."

She glances up at him, gobs of demon dung caking her rainbow hair, and wails loud enough to scare the dead.

"She's right," Crom says. "I can't take notes under these conditions. Plus, I think this place has permanently ruined my sense of smell. We have to find a way out of here."

"Speaking of," Spuck says as he ineffectively pulls on the cruddy bars of their cell. "Where the fraiche is Na-nu? That little arghole probably sold us out for a spit sandwich, or whatever demons like."

Ham, who has been quietly flickering as he rocks back and forth on the soiled floor, suggests, "Let's just put on another memory, and maybe this will all go away."

"Nah, that never works," Adam says, pacing the putrid cell.

"I bet Pants Team Pink would know what to do," D'ohry whimpers.

"If I have to hear one more word about Pants Team Pink, I'm going to…" But before Adam can think of a fate worse than the one they're currently experiencing, he hears a faint squishing sound heading down the corridor. Leaning as close to the chitty bars as he dares, he waits for the guard to approach and finally glances down to find a puddle of monster poop pooling under him. "*Aww*, not again."

The kids cry out as their spirits are seized and dragged out of the cell, but the guards are immune to the pitiful pleas. Before long, they enter a great hall lined with obscene statues and vaguely pornographic tapestries stained with feces. The monsters defecate their captives in front of the lumpy throne, and once the flatulence disperses, Adam and his students woozily glance around the room to find a familiar lesser demon looking down at them from the dais with a big chit eating grin on his face.

"Hey guys," Na-nu greets them, like nothing happened.

Charging the platform, Adam grabs the kid by his suspenders and shouts, "You tricked us, you little chit!"

"Very good!" an otherworldly voice announces, accompanied by a wet clapping that causes the old scrapper's stomach to spasm. "You're going to fit right in around here, space pirate."

Even though he hasn't performed the act since he was alive, Adam gets the sudden urge to empty his bowels as the hooded figure steps toward him. The demon looks like it just crawled out of a space sewer, its face and robes crusted with eons of dirt and grime. But underneath all the filth, Adam can detect the faintest hint of a peculiar aura.

"You know, we could have walked," the old scrapper says, gagging as one of the chit monsters standing guard behind the throne relieves itself in its malformed paw and slurps up the black mess. "You didn't have to drown us in chit."

Little flecks of dried filth crack from the demon's lips as it grins, the contours of its chit-covered face just visible beneath the hood of its soiled robe. "Where's the fun in that?" As the creature steps toward them, Adam sets Na-nu down and plants himself between the two of them. "Don't worry, I would never hurt little Na-nu, even if he is an annoying little spit. After all, there was a time when I was the only demon who would give him a place to squat."

"Who the fraiche are you?" Spuck asks?

Raising its arms, the demon announces, "I am the Argh Lord, and this is my kingdom. A receptacle for all the hate and misery that flows through Other Side, it was once believed that nothing could be built upon the 'sewer of the dead.' But I showed them."

"Good for you," Adam says. "So, are you the one who has my tapes, or what?"

Bowing its head, the Argh Lord casually wanders down the steps of the dais and around the hall, paying no attention as its bare, crud-covered feet splash through thick puddles of monster poop. "It's true that I have recently come into possession of a set of rare death tapes. When I caught Na-nu flashing his goods outside the Ghost Bar, I decided it was time he repaid me for my hospitality."

"Well, I want them back," Adam says.

"And I want to give them to you," the Argh Lord says. "The thing is, there are a whole lot of demons out there who would do revolting things to get their claws on just one of the deaths of Asteroid Jones. And now I've got them all." When the demon notices the death grip Adam has on his bag, it laughs and shakes its head. "Don't worry. I have no interest in your tapes, except as a bargaining chip."

Even as part of him is relieved, another part rolls its eyes and groans. "What does that mean?"

"It means I want to make a trade," the Argh Lord says. "There is a mysterious being that has been wreaking havoc in the Forest of Lost Souls. The only one of my scouts to have returned informs me that the creature is extinguishing spirits at an alarming rate, and now it seems to be headed in this direction. So far, no demon has been able to stop it, but I suspect the infamous space pirate Asteroid Jones may be up to the task."

Scoffing, Adam complains, "How am I supposed to do that?"

"Fraiche if I know," the demon says. "But if you pull it off, the tapes are yours. In the meantime, you'll understand if I hold onto your bag, just until you get back."

"No way," Adam says, clutching his collection tight. "It was hard enough getting the one back. I'm not letting them out of my sight."

The demon scowls, circling the kids. "Fine, but you'll have to leave the rest of these young souls as collateral. I'll permit you to take one of them so that there's someone to report back in case you lose yours."

"Mr. Jones would never leave us here," Cromula says, hopefully.

Glancing between his tapes and his horrified students, Adam says, "You understand, right? They would never survive in these conditions. I'll only be gone for a little while. You'll be okay." While Crom would be the obvious choice to assist him, he finally decides, "Come on D'ohry. The sooner we get this over with, the sooner we can get out of this chitsty."

As the once-plucky girl raises her watery eyes, Spuck cries, "You're taking *her*? That's it. We're doomed, for real this time."

# 82

"See, aren't you glad we came?" Grandpa asks as we peruse the finest specialty ration and fried dessert stands The Park has to offer.

"I guess," I mumble through a mouthful of confetti cake-wrapped carnival dog. "It's just, everything is different now." The best vacations of my life were spent at The Park. But I don't see any of the old booth jockeys, and all the best death traps have been 'upgraded.' Even the Rotor Man has been replaced by a newer model. I can sometimes still catch a glimpse of the old days amongst the ghosts of the Jungle Gym, but it's not the same.

"Yeah well…" Grandpa waves his melting green moon cheez log over the packed aisle. "Despite what their slogan would have you believe, even the Jungle Gym changes. You should have seen this place when your grandmother and I used to bring your father. Back then, there were no rules."

"You never talk about her," I mention between sips from my collectible Parkiversary cup. Somehow it seems easier to broach the subject at a time like this. "Dad used to mention her sometimes, but I still don't know much about her."

Lowering his cheez log, Grandpa gazes out at the hordes of cosplay crusaders, and the air around him turns misty. "She was one of the infamous Barbeau clones, a tough old scrapper. We raised Kren together, most of the time just scrapping by. Things were harder back then. A lot of our choices we made out of necessity. Even though she never said it, I always knew she was too good for a life in Misery Acres. When your father was old enough to scrap on his own, I urged her to go somewhere where she could pursue her dreams. We kept in touch over the space years. She passed not long before you were born." Wiping the tears away, he smiles and says, "I'll be right back. I'm gonna go get some more frosting for my cheez."

For a brief moment, in a way that's hard to describe, the universe between us seems to evaporate. But the feeling soon passes, and as the crowded booths rematerialize around us, I tell him, "Sure thing."

While he waits to get topped off, I stroll down the aisle, past heckling death predictors and Skee-Ball hustlers, and suddenly I'm really glad I came. Despite all the little differences, deep down it's still the same Park I remember. I guess someday everything will change, but not yet.

I close my eyes to soak in the joyful chatter and singular stench of Con City, when I feel myself crash into and nearly tumble over a glittery creature half my size.

"Watch it, you dumb drunk space pirate!" the little princess says.

"Hey, that's… accurate."

When she looks down and sees the beer stain on her sparkling gown, she screams, *"Mom, this chidiot ruined my dress!"*

"Nah, it'll come out," I assure her. "And even if it doesn't, I hate to be the one to tell you, but princesses are out."

"You're going to wish you hadn't said that." Digging her sneakers into the dirt, her glittery hair floats up off her shoulders, and her star wand crackles. A vicious smile stretches across her face, and with a dramatic twirl, my vacation is vaporized.

"Why did you have to pick me to come with you?" D'ohry complains as she trudges through the dense underbrush, the blinking lights on her sneakers barely visible beneath a thick layer of monster dung. "I mean, I don't want to be back there in the spit, but I can't catch a monster. I barely passed Universal History! You should have brought Crom. She got a perfect score on the life entrance exam."

Pushing aside the leafy branch of an unusually lively ghost wood tree, Adam says, "If you had been paying attention to what I just showed you then you would know that sometimes the most incredible power comes in the whiniest packages."

"Is that supposed to make me feel better?" she moans, the luster of her rainbow hair having faded dramatically since they set off on their journey.

"What I mean is, people aren't always as pathetic and helpless as they appear. Sometimes it just takes the right annoying scrapper to bring it out of them." Adam huffs ether as the Forest of Lost Souls gradually transforms into a ghost wood jungle. He does his best to stick it out, but before long, the pain in his old joints forces him to stop beside a petrified log covered in bright yellow ivy. "Let's rest here for a while," he says as he hoists himself up.

D'ohry pouts, and plopping down amongst the bright shrubs, she absently picks at the dead plant matter covering the forest floor. "We're never going to get out of this place, are we? Even if we do find the monster, it's just going to eat our souls, and the others are going to be stuck in that spit castle for the rest of eternity."

"She's right, you know," a 'spooky' voice chimes in, and Adam's ghost materializes to taunt him. "You're never going to make it."

"Don't listen to that ackle," Adam tells her. "The monster is around here somewhere. We'll just have to catch it before it catches us."

"Oh okay, no problem," she says, rolling her eyes.

While they recuperate in the shadow of the ghost wood, Adam can't help thinking that, in some backward way, he might bear a morsel of responsibility for their current plight. If he had just let the demons have his videos, maybe the class would be safe on the other side of the forest by now. On the other hand, those tapes contain some of his most formative deaths, without which he wouldn't be the same space pirate his students and the rest of the inhabitants of Other Side have come to know and worship. "And in the end, isn't that what this is all about?"

D'ohry lifts her frizzy head, and with a puzzled expression, she says, "What?"

"Nothing." As he ponders the current market value of their souls, he hears something rustling amongst the lost souls somewhere not far off, and he says, "Chut up for a space second."

"I didn't say anything…"

The sound grows louder as whatever is producing it barrels toward them, and soon the bushes directly across the clearing start to rustle. Before the monster spots them, Adam pulls D'ohry behind the ancient log he was sitting on and holds his finger over his mouth. A sickly thing with pasty green skin and a round potbelly, the monster charges into the clearing and wanders around sniffing the ether with its wide, snot-crusted nostril. Frantically scanning the trees through bulging, bloodshot eyes, it stomps the life out of everything that happens to get caught underhoof, until it finally gets bored and plops down on the forest floor.

"How the freak are we supposed to catch *that*?" D'ohry whispers indignantly. "It'll tear through us like holy paper."

"Is that like TP?" Adam asks and then shakes his head. "Forget it. We need to build some sort of cage or dig a giant hole for it to fall into."

"Are you serious?"

"I knew you were never going to make it," the ghost announces, instantly attracting the attention of the monster.

"Chut up, you chidiot!" Adam whisper-shouts.

But it's too late. The monster is already on its feet and cautiously plodding toward their log.

Trembling, D'ohry asks, "What are we going to do?"

"Fish it," Adam says. "When I stand up, you run. If you make it back, just remember to blame this all on BM."

"*What?!*" she cries. "No!"

"Don't worry, that ackle has it coming," the old scrapper says. "Just look after my tapes, will you?" He slips his bag from around his shoulder and passes it to her. Mentally bidding his memories farewell, he prepares himself for a serious goring, when the annoying ghost suddenly floats out ahead of him into the clearing.

"You're so not going to make it," it moans.

When the monster spots the lost soul, it leaps forward, gnashing at the ether. But its impractically large fangs just pass through the wandering spirit without effect. Tilting its head, the monster gives the ghost one more halfhearted swipe for good measure and then gives up.

"That dumb ghost actually did something good for once," Adam says. "Although, I kind of hoped it would get eaten. Anyway, I'll take those tapes back."

Shaking, D'ohry shoves the bag over to him, and one of the tapes shifts, producing an unnatural *clack*. The monster instantly perks up, and a moment later, it's lunging toward their log.

"Rat farts!" Adam cries, and shoving his bag back into D'ohry's hands, he jumps up to run for his afterlife. But upon seeing the monster's slavering slack jaw, he freezes in terror. Powerless to stop the soulthirsty beast, he gazes into the dark abyss of total annihilation, when someone turns on the light.

# 83

Standing outside the Misery Acres beverage store, surrounded by a rowdy gang of local scrappers as Ferd adds four drops of illicit UE military-grade nuclear bitters, the most ever attempted, to the glowing yellow orb in the center of my palm, I can't help but wonder if this is how it all ends.

"Come on, do it already," somebody shouts, and it's just the heckling I need to pressure me into popping the neon candy into my mouth.

The instant the ultra sour ball hits my tongue, my lips collapse in on themselves, and I drop to the moon pavement, where I proceed to writhe in bittersweet agony.

"He's having a sour seizure!" a girl screams.

Holding the crowd back, Ferd tells them, "He'll be fine. Just give him a space minute."

But as I involuntarily wriggle along the dusty sidewalk, gazing up into their worried faces, I'm not so sure. Unable to feel my face, I fear I may end up in a candy coma, never to recover, when the sour coating finally surrenders its sugary core. Once my senses return, I climb back onto my feet and crunch through what's left of the sour ball to cheers from all the grungy spectators – except for the ones who bet against me.

"All right, all right," Ferd tells them. "Show's over. You'll have a chance to win your crits back next space week, when Adam and I will be hosting the annual scrapper drinking contest. If you're underage, remember to get your parents to sign your permission slips. Until then, get the fish out of here." Once the crowd has dispersed, he presses his thumb onto my phone to transfer half the take and asks me, "How'd it go?"

I give myself a once over, and with the exception of a little candy reflux, I feel fine. "Easiest crits I ever made."

"This could be the greatest racket we've ever gotten into," he says. "Well, I'm going to take off. There's a UE fire damage sale calling my name – '*Ferd*!' Sure you don't want to come?"

"Next time," I tell him, and we jut our thumbs at each other as we part ways.

As soon as I step inside the store, my stomach starts churning, so I dig through the discount rations for something to settle it. As usual, none of the options on top of the pile are particularly appetizing, but I figure maybe if I search deep enough I'll find an old mystery loaf or moon cheezsteak.

I've got my head buried in the bin, when a vaguely familiar angelic voice says, "That was real impressive, what you did out there."

One of my adoring fans, I realize, and lifting my head, I say, "Thanks for watching. I—" But the moment I lay eyes on her, I lose my train of thought.

"I never thought I'd see anything so incredibly chidiotic," the girl says, smirking. "I don't know if you remember me…"

Even without the cartoon eyes and other digital mods, I'd recognize the spikey-haired cyber girl anywhere. "Jexxy_Silverstar," I whisper.

She laughs and hands me a ration, but I'm too distracted by the way the flickering shop lights accentuate her electronic ear to notice what flavor it is. Before I can reach the counter to pay, she stuffs the tray under my shirt and drags me out of the store as the owner chases after us, shouting a long string of alien profanities.

As we escape together across the parking lot, she yells, "Ciao, space pirate!" But before she runs off to find her ship, she grabs me by the vintage MATV Second Cousin of the Ghoul t-shirt and presses her soft purple lips to mine.

"It was wet, it was clumsy, and I never saw it coming," Adam says, shielding his eyes from the brilliant light illuminating the forest. "My whole nervous system just sort of seized up."

"Can we talk about this later?" D'ohry pleads from the shelter of their ghost wood log, her sneakers blinking wildly as the ground shakes beneath them.

"There might not be a later," Adam argues.

"Exactly!"

There's a pause in the scuffle, and Adam peeks over the top of the log as their pasty predator is wrestled to the ground by a strange humanoid radiating pure light. The monster howls, struggling to escape, but the light form has the beast outmatched. Wrapping its luminous limbs around the demon's gnashing head, the light whispers something too faint to make out, and the howling abruptly ceases.

"Wait!" Adam cries, but it's too late. The monster stops thrashing, and as the old space pirate watches its body dissolve into pure spirit and float up into the ether, he would swear he could make out a hint of a smile on its crusty face. "Come on," he says, pulling D'ohry along. "Let's get out of here."

The light fades behind them as they sprint back through the dark forest. But they're not fast enough, and in a moment, the light form overtakes them.

Blinded by its intensity, Adam falls to his knees to beg for their afterlives, when a celestial voice asks, "Who the fraiche are you guys?"

"We are but a couple of lowly lost souls with sensitive light receptors," Adam says, squinting.

"Oh, sorry." As the light surrounding the being softens, the pair discover a young translucent angel with a bush of seafoam hair staring down at them quizzically. "How's that?"

"Better," Adam says. "But I could use a beer." Thinking of a frosty can of Ol' Guard, an honest to Rodney cold one suddenly manifests in his hand, and before he has time to question his luck, he gulps it down.

"You don't look like the typical ghosts that haunt these woods," the angel says. "You seem more like… tourists. What are you doing out here? Don't you know how dangerous it is?"

Helping D'ohry to her feet, Adam says, "We're beginning to get an idea."

As the angel steps around the clearing, its bright aura gives new life to everything it touches. Eons of petrification in the ghost wood are miraculously reversed, and the forest floor grows thick with colorful vegetation as the dead plant matter soaks up the divine light.

"Why didn't you want me to free that demon's soul?" the angel asks.

"Because catching it is the only way to save my tapes… and our friends," Adam says. "They're being held by a powerful demon who sent us out here to trap a soul-eating monster. Although, something tells me you're the one the demon is really after."

For one of the all-knowing, the angel looks utterly perplexed. "What kind of demon?"

"It's some chithead called the Argh King," Adam explains. "It lives over in the Swamp of Asses."

"Swamp of Asses?"

"You know," Adam says. "It's that sewer down by the edge of the forest."

Scratching its scruffy head, the angel says, "This all seems very… what's the word?"

"Dumb?"

"That's it."

Just now taking notice of the angel's holy jeans and t-shirt, Adam asks, "Who the fish are you, anyway? And what are you doing out here? Shouldn't you be preparing new souls for life in the universe, or something?"

"Angels are free to administer salvation in any way they see fit," the light form says. "I prefer to tackle the problem at the source. A longer time ago than your spirits can possibly comprehend, one of my siblings got lost in these woods, never to return. It was then that I took a vow to purify this forest, one lost soul at a time. The name's Spitkicker."

"This is, like, really interesting and everything," D'ohry interjects. "But are you going to help us save our friends or what?"

"Hmm…" Plopping down on the lush forest floor, the angel gazes off into the ether.

"What are you doing now?" Adam asks.

"Thinking."

"Oh, that's just *great*," the old scrapper says. "We're wasting precious… well, not time exactly. But pretty soon I'm going to start getting bored."

"*Aww*," D'ohry moans. "I wonder what Pants Team Pink would do in a situation like this."

Perking up, the angel says, "You know Pants Team Pink?"

"*You* know Pants Team Pink?" Adam complains. "How?"

"I still have remote access to the universe," the light form says, scoffing. "I keep myself apprised of the latest trends. I'm not some new soul. No offense."

"I'm sure Pants Team Pink will save us all, some space day," Adam grumbles, taking advantage of the angel's regenerative light to snatch another beer from the ether. "But they're not here now, so we're going to have to figure this out on our own. Even with an angel on our side, it's going to take a miracle to get my tapes back."

"*Yes!*" the angel declares.

"You thought of something?" Adam asks, hopefully.

"Well, no," the light form says. "But as a fellow spiritual member of Pants Team Pink, your sparkly companion has convinced me to help you."

"Oh…," the old space pirate says, slumping. "Good, I guess. By the way, what did you whisper to that demon back there to free its soul?"

But the angel just smiles and shakes its head. "You wouldn't understand."

"If the team was here, they would work together to save their friends," D'ohry tells them, her rainbow aura intensifying as she paces inside the angel's bright sphere of influence. "They know that with teamwork, there's always a way to…" A sly, almost humanoid smile forms on her angelic face, and holding up the Pants symbol, she announces, "I have an idea, you guys!"

# 84

"Hey there, space pirate," Jexxy calls to me from across the pink sands of the parking lot.

Dressed in a short moon skirt and vintage jacket covered in alien band patches, she's wearing her hair down for a change, and as she pulls one of the long strands behind her modded ear, I tell her, "You look—"

But before I can find the words, she locks her mouth onto mine for a sloppy, gratuitous kiss.

When we finally pull our faces apart, she says, "I got you something." Digging around in her purse, a small glittery bag with a cartoon fish head printed on the front, she emerges with an old cruddy space pipe.

"You smoke space?" I ask.

"You mean, you don't?" she says, snickering.

She uses a squeeze lighter disguised as a pooping unicorn to melt the red tar in the bottom of the pipe, and inhaling deep, she blows the smoke into my mouth.

Except for the edges of the universe getting a little wobbly, I tell her, "I don't feel anything."

"Sometimes it takes a space minute," she says, grabbing my hand. "Come on."

Jexxy drags me to the entrance of the abandoned UE outpost turned clandestine space club, and I press my thumb to the disinterested door slug's credit pad to pay for our tickets. The out-of-tune crashing of unidentifiable scrap instruments reverberates through the building as we step down a long hallway plastered with torn posters and alien graffiti. When we reach the main room of the old moon station, we wade into a sea of sweaty scrappers thrashing to space punk renditions of their favorite TV theme songs.

"*I don't recognize this one*," she shouts over the bubbly rocker.

"*It's The Tra La La Song*," I tell her. "*But you might know it better as One Banana, Two Banana*."

"*Oooh...*," she says, jutting her thumb at the band of scrappy Earth-descendants banging out the hits up on the cramped stage.

The recycled air is so thick with the scent of space that I can actually feel it coating my tongue, and I start to get lightheaded, licking my dry lips as the crowd writhes around me.

"*You don't look so good,*" Jexxy says, but when I turn to face her, there's a big furry humanoid unicorn grinning at me in her place. "*Maybe you should get a beer. I programmed us fake IDs.*"

"Yeah, that's what I need," I mumble, "a cold one." But as she lifts my arm to apply the fake fingerprint, I discover that my hands have morphed into furry costume paws. Frantically yanking at them, I cry, "The paws won't come off!"

When the song is over, the band's flocked, bulbous-headed leader asks, "You guys got any requests?"

Gasping for breath inside my giant head, I look up to find that the entire audience has transformed into living cartoon characters, and I scream, "*What's happening?!*"

The crowd goes quiet for a moment to gape at me, and the singer finally says, "Yeah, we can play that one."

"At first I thought I smoked some bad space," Adam says, shaking off the memory as he puts his tape away. "But after I died I found out the club was way over capacity and the ancient CO2 converter couldn't keep up." He waits for D'ohry and the angel to comment, but when neither of them does, he bristles. "Are you even paying attention?"

"*Ye-es*," D'ohry whines, her sparkling aura restored from trudging inside the angel's divine light. "It was very educational."

"Oh yeah, then what happened?" he quizzes her.

"You had a bad date."

"Lucky guess."

"I don't know," Spitkicker says, leaving a vibrant trail of life in its path as it steps through the dead forest. "It seemed like everything was going okay until the end. I could stand to watch another one…"

But as Adam excitedly reaches back into his bag for the next tape, D'ohry cries, "No! We're almost there. I can smell it."

Before long, they find themselves at the edge of the ghost wood, gazing out at the great poop palace plopped in the bowl of the dark sewer. Setting D'ohry's plan into action, the angel suppresses its bright aura and puts on its demon disguise. But despite its best incorporeal contortions, it still looks sort of angel-y.

Giving the light form a once over, D'ohry says, "Yeah, that looks... bad, which I guess is good."

They briefly worry the angel will give itself away with all the life growing in its wake, but as they plod through the sewage, they quickly discover that even Spitkicker's divine powers are no match for the Swamp of Asses. By the time they reach the palace gates, the angel is covered in so much monster feces that it could almost pass for the Argh Lord itself. But just to be sure, Adam and D'ohry heap the black muck over its head and back until they've covered every trace of its divine origin.

"This is so humiliating," the angel mumbles inside its poop costume.

"How do you think I feel?" Adam asks. "I don't like to brag, but I'm *the* Adam Jones."

"*Oh...,*" Spitkicker says. "What does that mean?"

"Uh, I'm sort of a big deal." The old space pirate scoffs and nudges his student. "I don't blame you for not recognizing me. I've aged quite a bit since my heyday. But surely if you've heard of Pants Team Pink then you must be familiar with *Asteroid Jones*."

Shaking its soiled head, the angel says, "It's not ringing a bell."

Before Adam can express his discontent over this revelation, the palace guards rise from the sludge to drag the weary souls into the throne room. Except this time, with a little chit talking, Adam manages to convince them to let him and D'ohry escort their prisoner personally.

They do their best not to breathe as they trail the monsters downwind through the bowels of the palace, and as soon as they enter the moist hall, Cromula cries, "You came back!"

"Was there ever any doubt?" Adam asks.

Confined with the rest of his students inside a creature composed of living waste, she says, "Uh… no."

Up on the dais, the Argh Lord rises from its fecal throne and smiles down upon them through the hood of its grimy cape. "I never actually thought you would succeed." Plodding through poop puddles, the demon approaches the captive and says, "So, this is the demon that's been messing with the unnatural order around here. But how did you manage to capture what so many badargh others could not?"

Scowling at the grotesque creature, Adam says, "I may not be as spry as I once was, but this space pirate still knows a trick or two. So, are you gonna let my tapes and students go, or am I gonna have to unleash the full might of my magical scrapper powers on you too?"

"You're scaring me, space pirate," the Argh Lord says, hawking up a laugh. "Now that there's nothing left to impede the growth of my kingdom, I have no more use for you." Reaching into the pocket of its robe, the demon hands Adam his video and waves its cruddy paw at the guards holding his students, causing the monsters to melt away.

"Thanks…," Adam says, holding the soiled tape with his fingertips.

But as the demon leans in to get a closer look at the angel's face, it frowns. "There's something very familiar about this monster."

Lifting its head, the dirty angel stares the demon in its brown eyes and whispers, "Fartknocker."

A look of terror comes over the Argh Lord, but before the demon can escape, the angel leaps up and wrestles it to the floor. Restraining the evil arghole, Spitkicker furiously scrubs at its face, and a brilliant light shines out from underneath all the chit.

"Sibling," the angel says, and wiping away the muck to reveal its own true face, it wraps its arms around the squirming demon. "I finally found you."

"Get off, you stupid spitiot," Fartknocker growls, shoving the light form away. "Did it ever occur to you that maybe I didn't want to be found?"

"Nonsense," Spitkicker says. "You can't possibly enjoy living in this sewer. Now, collect your things and we'll get you back to paradise."

Yanking its arm away, the wannabe demon says, "But I like it here. In this place, I'm free to shape the spit in my own image. I'm not going back, and you can't make me."

"We'll see about that."

"It seems like you two have a lot to argue about," Adam says, motioning for D'ohry to guide the rest of the dazed students toward the door as the light forms' disagreement threatens to turn violent. "We'll just get out of your way." But when he goes to put his cruddy tape back in its holder, he cries, "Wait a space second, I'm still missing a tape!"

"Are you counting the one Daizy took?" Crom asks as she picks the dried chit out of her once glowing green hair.

"Yes I counted that one!" Adam cries as he counts them again. "Either that fishing demon or angel or whatever it is still has one of them, or Na-nu gave it away to some other chithead." He glares at the lesser demon shaking in his overalls, but the kid just shrugs.

"*Ack ack ack*," Fartknocker cackles, bearing its chit-stained fangs. "I know where it is," the angel-turned-demon taunts the old space pirate, conjuring traumatic memories of pink, phone-based board games, "*but I'm not telling.*"

# 85

Lying next to the virtual girl of my dreams as we watch the lights of the heavy weekend traffic flit around the ancient rock field from the captain's chair of my very own ship, I can hardly believe my luck. I figure nothing in the universe could be better than this, when Jexxy lifts her head and whispers, "I have a surprise for you."

"I hope it's not space," I tell her. "By the way, have you seen my Chibi Sitcom cards? I can't find them anywhere."

"Uh, no...," she says as she pads to the back of the ship. When she returns, she's carrying a six pack of something called Cud Xtra. "I swiped some beers from my parents' fridge."

"You know the way to my heart." Cracking a stolen one, I take a sip and wince. "It's no Ol' Guard. But it'll do."

"Scoot over, will yuh?" As Jexxy squeezes in next to me, she guzzles part of her can, leans in close, and belches.

The warmth of her body is an antidote to the cold, harsh universe outside. When I'm with her, there is no past, or future. There is only now.

"I belch you too," I tell her, and when I flip off the lights, the dark cabin is bathed in starlight.

For a long while, we gaze out at the twinkling lights, listening to each other breathing. Maybe it's because I've got Cud on the brain, but I think if I had one wish, it'd be to live in this moment forever.

"This thing is so itchy," she announces, yanking at her space suit. Silhouetted against the ship's window, she removes the dusty top, and when she lies back down, the only thing between me and her Ellie Mays is a thin layer of artificial fabric. "Now I'm cold."

She smells like sugar and space as she snuggles up against me and presses her face into my neck, sending a shiver through my body that causes me to drop my beer. Laughing at my loss, she begins peppering me with kisses, and the next thing I know, we're swapping spit.

My heart races as we squirm against each other in the dark, searching for a comfortable position. Pulling me closer, she feels around under my t-shirt, but as she tries to tear it off, I end up stuck with my arms around my head. A prisoner of my own shirt, I can her fingers brush my naked chest.

"What's so funny?" she asks, as I wriggle around the seat, halfheartedly trying to free myself from her giggling clutches. "Don't try to resist. You'll only make it harder on yourself." I can feel her tickle assault gradually heading south, until it arrives at my waist, and as she unbuttons my shorts, she says, "I wonder where else you're ticklish."

When she slips her hand down the front of my space jockeys, her fingers are so cold that I jerk out of my seat and into the dash, sending the ship into a tailspin.

After a moment of awkward silence inside the soiled hall, Fartknocker says, "Despite your torturous attempt at mating, I'm still not going to tell you where the tape is."

"This is no time for love, Mr. Jones," Spuck says, lifting his sunglasses. "Tape or no tape, let's get the fraiche out of this toilet."

"Well, I liked it," Ham notes, and when the others glare at him, he shrugs. "I mean, it wasn't my favorite…"

But as the kids move toward the exit, Adam cries, "We can't give up now. We've come too far to leave without my tape!"

"Aww, just tell them where it is," Spitkicker says, and in a flash, the angel has its unsanitary sibling in a spiritual lock. "Don't make me do this."

Struggling to wrench its robed head free, Fartknocker shouts, "Fraiche you!"

"You asked for it," the angel says, and balling its fist, it administers the most humiliating of all the hallowed punishments – the divine noogie.

"*Aaargh!*" Fartknocker wails. "Fine, I'll tell you! Just get the fraiche off me." Tearing itself away from its holy sibling's clutches, the demon briefly looks as if it's going to unmake the space pirate, when its hate-filled scowl suddenly flips downside up. "I'll tell you where it is. But good luck getting it back. And by good luck, I of course mean *bad* luck." The demon breaks into a fit of gurgling laughter, but when Spitkicker cracks its glowing knuckles, the ruler of the Swamp of Asses caves. "I offered the tape up as a sacrifice to King Dead. By now, it's at the center of the labyrinth on top of the great demon's treasure pile."

"*King Dead?*" Crom cries. "Labyrinth? None of this is on the map. How are we supposed to find it?"

"I know where it is," the angel says, losing some of its brilliant luster, "more or less."

"*Ack ack ack!*" Fartknocker howls. "Yes, take them to the labyrinth. They'll never find their way back out."

Frowning, Spuck says, "Eh, butt up already, will you?"

"I truly hate to say it, but Fartknocker is right," Spitkicker laments. "The Labyrinth of the Dead is no place for young souls. It was constructed as a prison to hold the most powerful demon in all of Other Side. It's a place where even angels fear to tread. If you're thinking of challenging King Dead just for some memory tape, I urge you to reconsider."

Just when the old space pirate thinks things couldn't possibly get any worse, the ghost from the forest rematerializes to haunt him. "You're never going to make it."

"Precisely," the angel says.

Looking at his students' scared faces, Adam tells them, "I'm sorry, but I have to try."

The angel nods and smiles slightly. "So be it." Plodding across the open sewer, it motions for the kids and their teacher to gather close and instructs them to, "Grab on."

"You mean you can travel through the ether?" Adam says as he places his hand on top of the light form's powerful paw. "Buttmuncher told us it couldn't be done."

"It's an angel trick. Now, is everybody ready?"

But before they can leave, Na-nu, still cowering up on the chitty dais, squawks, "Wait, I don't want to come. I really love being in this place, surrounded by these spitheads."

"O-*kay*…," the angel says, confused.

"That means he wants to go with us," Adam translates, and waving at the lesser demon, he shouts, "Come on already!"

Fartknocker cackles as the group puts their hands together, but the demon chuts up when Spitkicker tells it, "I'll be back."

"Ha, like in that movie from Mr. Jones's life," Ham remarks.

But the angel just stares at the flickering kid. "I don't know what you mean."

Without warning, the class blinks out of and back into existence, and suddenly they're back amongst the wandering spirits of the ghost wood. As always, the trip makes Adam sick, and he leans against one of the petrified trees until his stomach settles. Spitkicker turns up its aura, restoring the class's energy as it banishes the darkness surrounding them, but this deep in the forest the light form's range is limited.

"I don't see any maze," Adam says as they huddle together inside the angel's little bubble of light. "Fish, I can barely see anything at all."

"The *labyrinth* is around here somewhere, but its precise location is always changing," Spitkicker explains.

"We're in the darkest part of the forest. My light can only push the shadows back so far. You'll have to stick close if you don't want to get lost out here for the rest of your afterlives, or pre-lives as the case may be. It could be a long time before we find—" But as the angel turns to lead them through the dark forest, it crashes into a ghostly wall erected between the trees. "Oh, here it is."

Feeling along the side of the glowing structure, they eventually come to a dark opening protected by no gate and no monsters.

"That's it?" Adam says. "We can just walk in?"

The angel laughs. "Of course. Getting in is easy. It's the getting out that's tricky. And now that I have shown you the way, I must take my leave."

"*You're not coming?*" the old scrapper cries. "My confidence about this whole thing was sort of dependent on you being around to save us."

"I'm sorry," Spitkicker says. "But I cannot go with you. Well, I could, but I really don't want to. Plus, I've got a lot of spit to clean up. Just know that whether you make it out or not, your bravery will be known all throughout Other Side."

"A lot of good that'll do us," Adam grumbles. "At least tell us what you said to that demon whose soul you freed outside the Swamp of Asses. Maybe we can use it against King Dead."

"You don't get it," the angel says. "Every soul is different. The one inside this maze will not be saved so easily." But when it becomes clear that the old space pirate isn't satisfied, the light form shakes its bright head and laughs. "Fine, I'll tell you. But you're not going to like it." Lifting its hand to bid the class farewell, the ancient being blows a loud raspberry and disappears into the ether.

Kicking the patch of dense brush where the angel was standing, Adam gripes, "Well that's just great. Now we're stranded out here. On the bright side, at least we finally got rid of that stupid ghost..."

But as he examines the oddly familiar phosphorescence emanating from the labyrinth walls, a dumb voice whispers, "You're not going to make it."

# 86

"Dam it." I can barely pay attention to the heads exploding in tonight's animated epic assault on the senses as I obsessively check my phone to see if Jexxy has answered my txt. She's supposed to fly over to my place tonight to watch an ancient Block Party Summer recording I found, but I haven't heard from her all space day.

Setting my phone down on the coffee table, I try to keep my eyes off the glowing screen. But before I can stop myself, I'm picking it up to call her, again.

After a few rings, I get her holo-message, *"This is Jexxy's phone. If it's an emergency, leave a message and I'll call you back. If it's not an emergency, why aren't you txting me like a normal humanoid?"*

"Hey, it's Adam again. I just wanted to see if you're still coming over tonight. If it makes any difference, the video I found has the original ancient Earth commercials. Anyway, I belch you."

As soon as I set my phone back down, it rings, and I eagerly snatch it up, but it's just Grandpa calling to check on me. Grinning up from the screen, he says, *"Hi, it's Grandpa."*

"I know," I inform him. "I can see you."

*"Well, what'd I say? Is it a classic or what?"*

"Oh yeah, the movie's great," I tell him, glancing at the nuclear wasteland depicted on the screen.

*"It's just too bad it's censored. But that's Earthlings for you. They always know how to ruin a good thing."*

"Yeah, well, what are you gonna do? Anyway, I gotta go before I miss the end."

*"Wait a space second,"* the old man says as his friends holler in the background. *"That's not the reason I called. Now if I could just remember what it was…"*

"You guys better not be messing with my stuff." I knew letting him take the ship was a bad idea. "I have everything just the way I like it."

*"Don't worry, your ship is in good hands, or my name isn't Silas Ichabod Jones,"* he says, as one of his friends lumbers in front of the camera slurping an Ol' Guard.

"Is he drinking my beer?" I cry.

*"I believe that's* my *beer,"* Grandpa says. *"Now I remember! I called to make sure you aren't smoking space."*

"Nani?! *Space?* Smoke? Me? *No.*"

*"I could smell it on you when you came in the other night. I don't want you sparking up around my collection. Space smoke is terrible for videotapes."*

"You're killing me, Gramps."

*"Just remember, if you smoke in my house, you're already dead."*

Glaring at him, I nod and hang up the call. But as soon as I set my phone down, it lights up again.

Frantically tapping the glass brick, I find a message from Jexxy. *"Sorry cant make it tonight"*

She couldn't even do me the courtesy of punctuation. Slumping onto the couch, I turn up the volume on the TV, but I can't crank it high enough to drown out my sorrow.

"I guess that's what beer is for," I figure.

But when I drag myself to the fridge to grab a cold one, I discover that Grandpa cleaned it out. I was saving the crust of tar in the bottom of Jexxy's space pipe to smoke with her. But since she's not coming, I plop down in front of the TV and light up.

"Turns out Grandpa was worried about more than just his tapes after all," Adam says. "Ever since we fixed the generator, he started cranking the oxygen. As soon as I lit the chitty beverage store lighter, it exploded, and one of the sparks landed on the old shag rug. The whole place went up like, uh… something that burns really fast."

Raising his hand, Ham suggests, "A fart?"

"Sure…"

"Good pep talk," Spuck cracks, gazing through his sunglasses into the dark entrance to the labyrinth, where even the lost souls haunting the ghost wood refuse to drift.

"In life, death lurks around every corner," Adam warns them. "Speaking of, I'm starting to think maybe you kids should wait out here. I'm an old soul. I've already done my fair share of living. But you still have a bazillion lives ahead of you."

"You're finally starting to talk sense," Spuck says. "We'll meet you back here if you ever make it out."

But as Adam moves toward the shadowy opening, D'ohry cries, "We can't just let him go in there by himself after all he's done for us!"

"The only thing that arghole has done is get us lost in this stupid never-ending forest, probably forever!" Spuck argues.

"Even so…" D'ohry glares at the boy, her rainbow aura flaring, and he backs down. "Mr. Jones showed me that just because I'm small and sparkly doesn't mean I'm not strong. Sure, we almost lost our souls a few times, and it was pretty much all his fault. But we're still here, aren't we? I think what he's been trying to teach us this whole time is how to unlock the true power hidden deep inside each and every one of us, just like Pants Team Pink!"

Glancing at his students dubiously, Adam clears his throat and says, "Not like Pants Team Pink. But, uh, yeah. Of course that's what I've been teaching you. If you couldn't see that, then maybe you're the arghole…"

"I'm with D'ohry," Cromula announces, and pulling up her map, she renames the place from Labyrinth of the Dead to Labyrinth of the Living Dead. "You know, like alive, which is good."

"I'm not sure that's any less bad," Adam says.

"Well, it's not supposed to sound inviting," she tells him. "Anyway, we haven't come this far just to Spuck out now. Plus, I have to see the rest of Mr. Jones's deaths." Shooting D'ohry an accusatory glare, she adds, "And I want to know what happened in the ones we missed while we were locked up in that spit palace."

Shrugging his pixelated shoulders, Ham says, "I'm in. The heroes never just give up and go home."

When even Na-nu opts to stick with the rest of them, Spuck groans, *"Guhhh... I don't want to stay out here all by myself!"*

With that settled, the six of them cautiously approach the opening, and Adam sticks his head in to look around. All he can make out are the vague outlines of the labyrinth's dark corridors, and as he debates whether he could stand to sacrifice just one of his deaths to avoid going inside, the walls start shaking.

"What the fraiche is happening?" Spuck asks.

"I think it's changing locations," Adam says. "Quick, everybody get inside before we lose it."

As they step over the invisible threshold, Adam hears a wispy voice taunt, "You're never going to—"

But when he turns around to tell the ghost to fish off, the entrance is walled up. Feeling around where the opening used to be, he cries, "We're trapped!"

"Now what are we going to do?" Spuck moans.

Squinting at the glowing walls surrounding them, Crom says, "Uh, guys, we might be in more trouble than we thought. This isn't regular ghost brick. These are spirit barriers."

When Adam looks really close, he can make out the pained expressions of tortured souls swirling inside the glowing stone. "Neat."

"You mean something trapped them in there?" D'ohry wails.

"Worse," Crom says. "Not even the most powerful demon has the ability to capture souls like this. The only way to create a spirit barrier is to give oneself willingly.

I've heard of that type of sacrifice, but I didn't think it had ever been performed. Whatever type of demon is being held in here was dangerous enough to compel all these souls to give up their eternal freedom to ensure it could never get out."

Throwing his hands up, Adam says, "Well, there's no turning back now. So, which way should we go?"

"Whatever we do, let's make sure we don't get lost this time," Crom says. "If we're not careful, we could end up walking in circles for eternity."

"How are we supposed to do that, *Cromula*?" Spuck asks.

"I don't know, *Spuckler*," she says. "Maybe we could use the *map*. I'll mark our path so we don't wind up retracing our steps."

"Good idea!" the boy says.

"I know!" she counters.

As they argue over which direction is least likely to lead them to eternal frustration, Adam turns away just in time to glimpse a familiar furry tail disappearing around the end of the passage, and he mutters, "Daizy?"

# 87

"That was the last time I heard from her," I tell Ferd as we wander the beverage store parking lot.

"Look on the bright side," he says, handing me a blue ration pop. "You still got ol' Ferd. That's gonna be three crits, by the way."

"But ration pops only cost two crits!"

Holding out a credit pad displayed on his phone, he says, "That's my premium for aiding and abetting a known ration thief. I'm providing a valuable service at great risk to my own shopping privileges. One day, when I open my own scrap shop, I'll let you park for free – on the condition that you can control your obviously insatiable urge to shoplift. But until then…"

"I'll look forward to that," I grumble, the ration pop melting down my hand as I press my thumb to the screen.

"In the meantime, there are plenty of cyber girls in the virtual sea," Ferd says, and glancing around the parking lot, he points to a group of kids gathered outside the store, surrounded by a dense cloud of space. "There's some now."

"It's not that simple," I moan, and as I scan the crowd, I see her.

Pulling her silver hair back over her modded ear as she smiles at some techno-punk covered in cheap electro implants, she inhales from his space pipe and blows out a puff of red smoke.

"That's her, isn't it?" Ferd says, and before I can stop him, he's charging across the moon pavement, shouting, "Hey you, Jexxy_Starfish or whatever." As soon as she sees me, her smile evaporates. "Do you have any idea how much you've cost this scrapper in shopping premiums alone? My services don't come cheap, although they are competitive."

"Adam…," she chokes, and I motion for Ferd to give us some space as we step away from the crowd.

Twisting her sneakers in the moon dust and glancing at me through wet eyes, she says, "I'm sorry. I didn't want to…"

"What happened?" I demand.

She refuses to make eye contact, crossing her arms as she turns away. "It's my parents. They said the only way they'll help me get my own ship is if I stop talking to you. They think you're a bad influence. I just thought this would be the easiest thing, for both of us."

For a brief moment, I'm too confused to respond to the allegations. "Did you tell them that *you're* the one who got us banned from the store?"

"Please!" she wails, stomping the sidewalk. "Don't make this harder than it already is."

"So that's it?" I ask. "You're just gonna quit talking to me?"

"*What do you want me to do?*"

"Tell them to fish off," I suggest. "We can live on my ship, and we'll scrap to get by. It'll be romantic."

Wrapping her arms around me, she plants her lips on mine one last time and whispers, "Ciao, space pirate."

"After that, I couldn't look at an exploding head without getting choked up," Adam tells his students as they navigate the dense fog suffusing the labyrinth's dark corridors.

Somewhere behind him, Spuck says, "Yeah, that's real sad and all. But where the fraiche are you taking us?"

"I thought I saw… something," the old scrapper says, anxiously adjusting his tape bag.

Striding alongside him through the maze, her sneakers flashing with a newfound confidence, D'ohry says, "This is why they call him Mr. Asteroid Jones. He can see things that others can't."

"We haven't run into any dead ends yet," Crom notes, following their path on her map. "Maybe the spirits of the labyrinth are guiding us in the right direction, or something."

Adam can just make out Daizy's dark shadow swimming in the haze up ahead, but no matter how fast he moves, he can't seem to catch up to her. Before long, he loses sight of her altogether, and he comes to a confused stop in the middle of the passageway. "I lost her. I mean, *it* – the trail."

"*You see?*" Spuck cries, his sunglasses cracked and covered in dirt. "He doesn't know what he's doing. It's a miracle we've survived this long, and now we're probably going to be lost for eternity because of him."

"Butt up, Spuck," Crom tells him. "We're not lost. We just don't know which way to go."

Hoofing it from behind, with Na-nu happily riding atop his pixelated shoulders, Ham says, "I don't mind taking a break."

"We're bound to find the center eventually," Crom says, consulting her map. "Let's just try one of these tunnels. But which one…"

As his students discuss their options, Adam glances out ahead and spots the shadow of a bushy tail waving at him from down the corridor. Without thinking, he charges into the fog and chases after the phantom.

"Wait!" D'ohry yells after him. "We have to stick together."

But by the time he looks back, the only thing he can make out are the dim lights from her sneakers flashing in the shadows. He knows he should stop, but he's afraid that if he does, he'll lose her forever. As he winds through the tunnels of the dark maze, it occurs to him that this is probably all just a trick to separate him from the others, but he can't help himself. He has to know.

Moving as fast as his old legs will carry him, he begins to fear he might never catch up to her, when she suddenly stops. Afraid of what he might find waiting for him in the dark, he halts his chase and calls, "Daizy?"

The figure moves toward him, and as he prepares himself to be torn asunder by the worst demon in Other Side, the love of his afterlife steps out of the fog. She looks exactly the way he remembers her, dressed in her power suit, her dark hair frizzed out around her triangle ears as she wraps her arms around him.

Purring with excitement, she cries, "I'm so glad you found me. I thought I was going to be lost in this place forever."

Adam sighs, resting his head against hers. "You don't know how happy I am to see you. But how did you end up in here? And why did you run away?"

"I asked some demon for directions on my way through the Forest of Lost Souls," she says. "The fish head told me I could take a shortcut through the labyrinth. I ran because I thought you were one of the monsters that live in this place, feeding on the lost souls that happen to wander inside."

Suddenly remembering his students, Adam prays they haven't run into any such monsters. "But how did you manage to survive?"

"Using my feline instincts, of course," she says. "Now, come on. We're getting out of here."

"What do you mean?" he asks as she pulls him along.

"I found a crack in the wall," she explains, impatiently dragging him down the tunnel. "I'm not strong enough to open it by myself, but with our energies combined, we should be able to break through."

Sure enough, they come to a wall on the outer rim of the maze with a large split down the middle. Adam doesn't even want to imagine the type of monster capable of damaging the spirit barrier, but it looks like it may have provided them with a way out. A shaft of bright light escapes from the crack, and Adam peeks through to glimpse the pastures of paradise waiting on the other side.

"Come on," Daizy tells him. "We have to do it together."

Concentrating all their energy into their hands, they lay their palms against the living dead wall and push. At first, it doesn't seem like it's going to budge, then all of a sudden, they hear a loud *crack*. Emboldened, they press their shoulders into the unbreakable barrier, and the wall crumbles.

"Come on!" Daizy shouts, running out into the divine light.

But as Adam gazes at the eternal dawn, he tells her, "Wait, I have to find my students first. It won't take long."

"They'll find their way," she assures him, reaching for his hand. "There's nothing to worry about."

"Maybe…" But as he stares down the dark tunnel, he can almost hear them searching. "I still need to find my death tape. It's the whole reason we're here. Once I have that, and the one you stole, my collection will be complete, again."

"You mean these?"

He turns back to find Daizy waving his tapes and he asks, "But how…"

"I have my ways," she tells him, and wrapping her arms tight around his neck, she drags her rough tongue across his cheek. "Now, let's go home."

# 88

Hauling last space week's garbage across the lifeless gray junkyard, I hurl the bag onto one of the countless putrid piles dotting the hostile moonscape, when Ferd's voice enters my helmet, *"Might as well do a little scrapping while we're here. I got a good feeling about this junk."*

"Careful," I say, watching him climb up the mountain of trash. "You don't want to cause—" But before I can finish warning him, one of the bags comes loose, and he tumbles back down amid a giant trashalanche. Once the garbage settles, I help dig him out and tell him, "Scrapper rule number… seven, I think – the good stuff is never on top."

*"That not true,"* he says as he rummages through a bag of old beer cans. *"Sometimes that's exactly where it is. Space hell, I bet these old cans are worth a few crits apiece, to the right collector."*

"Well, it's something like that," I assure him, and gazing out across the great trash dunes, I spot a suspicious glint that gets my scrapper sense tingling.

As we plod toward the mystery object, Ferd asks, *"So, are you coming to the grand opening?"*

"I wouldn't miss it," I tell him. "Since I got banned from the beverage store, the scrap has been piling up. I've got a whole heap of chit I need to unload."

*"Brule,"* he says. *"I could use the inventory. I'm planning to scale up fast. It won't be long before you can tell all the space girls that you're close personal friends with the owner of the biggest scrap shop in the galaxy."*

"I'm sure they'll be very impressed."

*"Speaking of, are you done moping over that cyber girl? What's her name, Jaffee?"*

"It's Jexxy, and I still think she might call."

Ferd groans into my helmet. *"Look at yourself. You barely eat, you're hooked on space, and you've stopped watching TV."*

"You're the one who brought me to Space Den!" I argue. "Plus, I don't have a TV to watch."

*"That's beside the point,"* he says, wiping the dust from his helmet. *"She's distracting you from a whole universe full of valuable trash."*

Jutting my thumb out, I announce, "Eh, you're full of chit."

But as we round a heap of gently exploded furniture, I lay eyes on the object of my salvation. There on top of the trash heap, amongst a treasure trove of barely used scrap, sits the TV and VCR of my dreams. They're older models, but they've obviously been cared for. Whoever dumped them even wrapped up the power chords so they wouldn't drag in the moon dust.

Gazing out over our find, Ferd grunts satisfactorily and says, "Told you."

Cutting the memory off, Adam asks, "Are you sure this is interesting? You never cared about my deaths before."

"Of course," Daizy says, staring at him with rapt attention. "I love watching your memories. So, how did you die?"

"Uh, I tried to force the TV's proprietary UE plug into the universal standard outlet on my ship and got electrocuted."

"Electrocuted," she says, shaking her head. "That's classic you."

"Um, yeah…"

Rubbing up against him as they stroll through the bright pastures of paradise, she wraps her tail around his arm and says, "That's one of the best things I've ever seen. Let's watch another one."

"Yeah, okay," he tells her, but as he reaches into his bag, he gets the feeling he's forgetting something. "Where are we going, anyway?"

"Where do you think? We're going home." Laughing, she points out ahead and says, "See, there it is."

Sure enough, if he squints hard enough, he can make out his little bubble of space way off in the distance. "Oh, right." Somehow he had forgotten. Everything that's happened since he left the house suddenly feels like a vague dream. Thinking back, he can barely remember how he escaped *the labyrinth*…

"My class!" he cries. "They still haven't found their way out. We have to go back and help them."

"Aw, they'll be fine," she says. "By the time we finish the next tape, you'll forget all about them."

She pecks his cheek, and he realizes that she's right, of course. He's just being paranoid. Still, he can't shake the feeling that something is wrong, and when he listens close, he would swear to Rodney he can hear someone calling his name.

"That's nothing," she tells him.

"What's nothing?"

Squeezing her arms around him, she pleads, "I want to watch another video."

"I can't believe I'm saying this," he tells her. "But my tapes can wait. If I lose those kids, Buttmuncher will never let me hear the end of it. Plus, I've grown sort of fond of them."

*"Don't leave me again,"* she suddenly wails, her tail tightening around his wrist.

*"You* left *me!"* he argues as he drags her back toward the labyrinth. "I'm sorry, but I have to *go…"* But the more he struggles, the deeper her claws dig into his soul, until he collapses onto the divine substrate.

*"Mr. Jones?"* a voice calls from the opening in the wall.

Adam tries to pull himself toward it, but with Daizy clinging to him, he can barely move.

*"Asteroid Jones…"* the cry echoes across the ethereal plane, and with his last shred of strength, he lifts his head to glimpse the kids racing toward him.

Ceasing his struggle, he laughs and tells Daizy, "You can let go. Now that we're all together, we can finally go home."

But his dreams of a long, quiet afterlife are shattered by the piercing howl that escapes her lips as his students proceed to give her a spirited pummeling.

"What the fish are you doing?" Adam chokes. "That's Daizy!"

"Wake up, space pirate," Spuck tells him, and reaching into the ether, the boy shoves a moldy can of Ol' Guard under the scrapper's nose. "That ain't Daizy."

The moment the rotten beer hits Adam's nostrils, the light inside the heavenly plane begins to fade, and the bright sky dims. The grass covering the lush pasture underneath him turns black as the shadows take hold, and suddenly he finds himself back inside his waking nightmare, surrounded by the living dead walls of the labyrinth. A sharp pain radiates through his soul, and he glances back over his shoulder to find his students furiously attacking his lower half.

"Stop," he mutters into the dirt. "Don't hurt—" But the words catch in his throat when he sees the scaly, bug-eyed monster biting down on his legs. A giant slimy fish head with razor teeth and chicken legs, it paralyzes him with its lifeless stare as it scrambles to swallow his soul.

"Don't worry," Crom says, as she batters the creature with her travel sack. "I think it's getting weaker."

The monster sinks its fangs into Adam's waist to keep him from slipping out of its dripping maw, and the old scrapper screams out in holy terror.

"Maybe not," she amends.

"Mr. Jones!" D'ohry cries, and planting her sneakers in the dirt, she tries to yank him out by his arm.

"This isn't working!" Spuck shouts, his imitation karate kicks proving largely ineffective against the fish head's thick scales.

Smashing his pixelated fists against the monster's fins, Ham says, "Don't worry, if there's one thing I've learned from Adam's movie collection, it's that something always saves the heroes at the last moment."

But when the fish bites into Adam's chest, he screams, "*Nothing is coming to save us!*"

As the hopelessness of their situation sinks in, the kids cease their attack and fall into sobbing.

"I'm going to miss you, Mr. Jones," Crom wails.

"*Me too*," D'ohry and Ham cry.

"Well, I'm not," Spuck says, but even with his eyes obscured behind his dark sunglasses, he can't hide his tears.

They huddle together for spiritual support as they bear witness to the end of Asteroid Jones, when a small voice calls out, "Maybe I can't save us." The crying abruptly ceases as the lesser demon, with his shaggy hair and overalls, carelessly scampers across the corridor. Even the monster seems disoriented, pausing its meal to turn one bug eye on the demon kid as he approaches. With a demented grin on his face, Na-nu reaches out his paw and gives the monster a vigorous itching behind the fin.

The fish head's legs spasm and its eyes roll back as the kid digs its claws in, and when he hits the sweet spot, the monster's jaw drops open, expelling Adam onto the cursed ground in a pool of slobber. As soon as Na-nu quits scratching, the creature hops around to face him, and it peels open its slimy fish lips to give the lesser demon a big thank you lick.

# 89

When I was a kid, my dad taught me that if you get a good education and try hard, you can do anything in life. I should have listened. But like my ex used to tell me, I've got no class.

Well, that changes now. My dream of attending space college is finally becoming a reality. I may be older than the average freshman, but I'm determined to make my way with the rest of them. It's like I always say, no matter how rich and successful a spaceman is, without an education, he's nothing.

It turns out registering for classes is worse than the space track, but the real inconvenience is showing up to them. No matter how hard I try, I just can't wrap my head around this stuff. The other kids may be book-smart, but I went to school in the real world.

My business teacher has *really* got it in for me. He might be good at manufacturing widgets in fantasyland, but he doesn't know the first thing about running a business. And don't get me started on my history professor. His interpretation of events depends on who screams the loudest.

But there is one upside. My literature professor is like a vision out of *Ulysses*. The sound of her voice transports me to another world, one in which her and I drink wine and eat cheese in a bright field surrounded by sheep.

Life on campus takes a little getting used to, *real little*. I don't even have to get out of my bathrobe, and the next thing I know, I'm getting asked to join the diving team. The coach apparently saw what I could do back at the Misery Acres pier, but I had to explain to him that even in my prime my signature dive almost killed me.

One night while I should be studying, Ferd and I head out to the local bar, and after a few pitchers too many, we somehow end up on the receiving end of the football team's tacklers. Except for Ferd's trigger finger and my hangover, the damage is moderate.

Of course, my studies begin to suffer a little from my late-night exploits, but when I explain to my professor how ill-prepared I am as a student, she takes pity on me and agrees to be my tutor. I open up to her like no one else I've ever met, and we spend a wild, passionate study session together. It all feels like some sort of celluloid dream.

All in all, student life suits me. In fact, my biggest problem is my dormmate. He always wants to do things the hard way. You hire Kurt Vonnegut to write one essay, and suddenly you're a monster. I'd tell him to take a hike if it wasn't for the fact that he happens to be my son.

"Wait a zeptosecond," Ham says, his pixelated body flickering in the dark tunnel. "This all sounds very familiar." Brow furrowed, he points his finger in the air. "That's not your life. It's that movie *from* your life. What's it called… *Back to School?*"

"Seeing *Back to School was* one of the great joys of my life," Adam mutters, his back propped against the labyrinth wall as he tries and fails to summon the energy to lift his broken soul.

"O-kay…," the boy says. "But how did you die?"

Thinking it over for a moment, the old scrapper finally shrugs. "I guess the generator probably broke down again or the dome got struck by a freak piece of space junk. Or maybe the movie was just *that* good. I don't know anymore."

Not far from where Crom is administering to Adam's wounds, Na-nu is playing fetch with the fish head that tried to swallow the old space pirate's soul. The lesser demon must have saved one of the squeak toys from the claw machine, and now the monster is acting like the kid's pet, chasing the rubber devilguy into the shadows and faithfully dragging the cursed toy back between its slimy lips.

"Do we have to keep that *thing* around?" D'ohry complains, jutting her nearly sparkleless thumb at the scaly creature. "I don't like the way its eyes jiggle around. Plus, it stinks!"

"I kind of like it," Spuck says, ripping the devilguy out of the creature's jaws. "Anyway, it never hurt anyone."

"It almost ate Mr. Jones's soul!" Crom cries as she finishes transferring some of her energy to the debilitated space pirate.

"Oh, right…" Winding back, Spuck whips the toy down the corridor, and the monster scurries off after it on its chicken legs. "Well, what the fraiche are we going to do now? We don't know what other monsters are hiding in these tunnels, and our fearless teacher can barely move. We're doomed, again."

"Butt up, Spuck!" Crom tells him. "If Mr. Jones has taught us anything, it's that there's always a way."

"Yeah, a way to fraiche things up," the boy says.

Ignoring him, she opens her map to scrutinize the dashed line indicating their path so far. "We'll be fine. We'll just have to split up. Half of the class can explore the labyrinth while the rest of us stay here with Mr. Jones."

Spuck thinks it over for a moment and decides, "That's *not* the dumbest idea I've ever heard."

While they argue logistics, Adam finds that Crom's healing is working, at least partially. Gathering his strength, he leans his shoulder into the wall, and with the sounds of countless trapped souls moaning in his ear, he somehow manages to get back on his feet.

As Crom prepares to lead Ham and Spuck back out into the stupid unknown, Adam chokes, "Wait…" D'ohry quickly runs over to help support his frail soul, but he assures her, "I can make it. We have to stick together."

"Aw, just stay here, old man," Spuck says. "You're only going to slow us down."

But the ancient space pirate is nothing if not stubborn. "This whole adventure has been trap after trap. Maybe the map is wrong or the walls are shifting or the labyrinth is infinite. All we know for sure is that we don't know anything. If we split up now, we might never find each other again."

His students don't say it, but he's taught them well enough to know he's right. The darkness seems to seep in as what little remains of their once-bright auras fades to an almost imperceptible haze. The only one who doesn't seem affected by the hopelessness of their circumstances is Na-nu. Even as the darkness surrounds him, he just keeps on playing with his stupid pet monster.

While the others wither under the weight of their fear, the demon kid tosses the evil toy down the dim passageway and giddily watches the giant fish head drag its flat nostrils through the dirt in pursuit. The act is so uniquely grotesque that it's mesmerizing. Before long, the creature comes running back to drop the toy at Na-nu's feet, and as Adam watches the ritual play out over, and over, and over again, he's struck with a sudden flash of divine inspiration.

But before he can announce his brilliant plan to save them, Crom says, "You have an idea!"

"*How did you know?*" he demands.

Pointing over his head, she says, "Your halo popped up."

"Anyway, I think I figured out a way to save us." Slipping his bag off his shoulder, he opens it and gets momentarily sidetracked gazing at its expertly organized contents.

"Your tapes aren't going to save us," Spuck finally says, snapping Adam back to reality.

"That's where you're wrong, I think." Taking his next death out of its case, Adam cautiously approaches the monster that almost ate him and holds the tape up to its smell hole.

As his plan dawns on the others, Spuck says, "Hey, you're not trying to get us out of here. You're just trying to find your tape!"

"One thing at a time," Adam says. "Once we have the tape, we'll have plenty of time to find a way out."

"But just look at that thing," Crom says as the creature's hideous tongue lolls out of its mouth. "How can we trust *that*?"

The old scrapper shrugs. "Can you think of a better idea?" As soon as the fish head has the death's scent, Adam pretend-hurls the tape down the passageway, and the monster takes off stumbling into the dark.

## 90

I can't do anything right. Even when I think I'm doing the right thing, I always find a way to fish it up.

Last night I was the king of the universe. I had it all – the grades, the girl, the gusto. But I flew too close to the sun. I was rightly accused of cheating on my exams, and now I only have a few space days to cram an entire semester's worth of information into my thick head.

The worst part is, my girlfriend flunked me. But I don't blame her. It's all my fault. I turned my back on everything I believe in.

Sometimes it seems like the only person looking out for me is Ferd. If it wasn't for him, I would've given up at the first hint of the letter 'F'. But with his help, I'm determined to show those professors, and myself, what I'm made of.

The following space days are a studying blur. I spend every waking and non-waking moment absorbing all the stuff I should have learned during the semester. By some miracle, I manage to convince my girlfriend to take me back, and she helps me study at double speed. I even take up the ancient practice of reading in the shower.

When the day of the big retest arrives, I can barely keep my eyes open, let alone cogitate. My head drooping, I do my best to follow along as my business teacher hits me with the single most complicated question ever devised. Fortunately, my professor girlfriend goes a little easier on me, and it's just what I need to fuel me through the rest of my exams.

The next thing I know, I'm meeting Ferd in the bleachers before the school dive meet. My head is spinning, and even though I successfully completed all my exams, I have no idea how poorly I did.

Then, just as I'm at my most tired and broken, a familiar voice calls upon me to fulfill a higher purpose. It's the coach. One of the divers got a bad cramp, and the team is in desperate need of a replacement. Having borne witness to my skills in the water show back at the Misery Acres pier, he wants me to sub in. I haven't been in the water in space years, and with my body, I politely decline. But Ferd goads me on, and suddenly I'm running off to the changing room.

I figure I must be out of my mind as I step out in front of the cheering crowd, but when I get to the top of the diving board, I check the wind, clear my pits, and take the plunge.

"That's *Back to School* again!" Ham cries, his aura flickering as he and Crom help Adam stumble down the dark passageway.

"I don't think so," Adam says, the fate of his old soul resting on their shoulders as it struggles to heal. "You must be thinking of the sequel that never was…"

He can hear the giant fish head furiously sniffing the walls of the labyrinth up ahead as it leads them Rodney knows where. While the rest of them do their best to keep pace with the monster, soon the only thing guiding the old space pirate and his two best students is the dim flashing of D'ohry's sneakers.

"We're going to lose them," Crom says, her green hair matted with sweat and grime. "And then we'll be stuck in this stupid maze forever."

"Look on the bright side," Adam tells her, patting his bag. "At least we still have my videotapes."

"But we've already watched most of them," she argues. "That means…"

"That's right," he says. "Enough reruns to last us all eternity."

"We can't let that happen," Ham moans. "Come on, we'll drag him if we have to."

The kids' auras brighten as they summon the strength to lift the old space pirate off his feet, and together they shuffle down the corridor as fast as their little legs will carry him. But it's not fast enough.

Shortly after losing sight of the others, Ham cries, "They might have gone down any one of these tunnels. I can't believe they just left us behind like that."

"I still have so many lives to live!" Crom whines.

As they approach the end of the tunnel, they suddenly come upon a dark obstruction hissing at them from the shadows, "*Shhh…*"

Startled, Crom and Ham thrust Adam's frail body out in front of them to absorb the blow from whatever demon trap they've fallen into now, when they stumble into a pile of familiar souls.

"Thanks a lot," Adam tells his two former best students as he picks himself up off the dead dirt.

"You're the famous space pirate," Crom argues. "You're better equipped to handle that sort of thing."

"What, dying?" he asks.

"Well, yes…," she says.

Looking at the nervous kids huddled inside the dark passageway, Adam questions, "So, what's the hold up?"

"This stupid fish head doesn't know where it's going," Spuck says, jutting his thumb toward the giant pet monster anxiously hopping around the next fork in the maze. "It can't make up its mind."

"It must have lost the scent," D'ohry posits. "But Na-nu will surely help us! After all, it's his pet."

The lesser demon gives the monster a vigorous fin scratch, and speaking in his native demon tongue, he tries to help it pick a direction. After an extended weighing of options the kid finally pats the goggling creature's head, and turns back toward the others.

"So, what's the problem?" Adam asks.

But the kid just shrugs.

"I bet Pants Team Pink would know what to do," D'ohry says.

"Yeah, I bet they would," Adam grumbles. "Maybe the fish head just needs to take another whiff." But as he searches his bag for one of his more pungent deaths, he pauses. "Do you guys hear something?"

They all grow quiet except for Na-nu's pet, frantically shuffling its chicken feet, and Spuck says, "It's like a squishing sound."

"Is it moaning?" Crom asks.

As the noise echoes between the labyrinth walls, Adam steps to the end of the passage and peeks down the next aisle, where he catches a brief glimpse of something big and slimy squirming in the shadows. Backing up into the wall, he whisper-shouts to the others, "*Wa-ahhh...*"

At his urging, the whole class frantically ducks down the next passage, and the fish head collapses onto the dirt, playing dead as the mystery monster makes its soggy approach. Squirming into partial view, the monster's dark, pulsating body hovers over its prey, a vague, globular shadow prowling the corridors. A soft glow illuminates its gelatinous innards, and as it moves closer to inspect the fish head, Adam realizes that the lights are actually lost souls writhing inside the beast's stomach. He wouldn't wish such a fate even on the annoying ghost that was following them around the forest, probably.

Adam prepares to make what he figures will be a futile run for it as the soul-eater reaches its gooey feelers toward the next aisle, when the monster suddenly loses interest and moves on, leaving a thick trail of glowing green slime in its wake. As the sounds of the creature's moist movements fade back into the labyrinth, the fish head jumps back onto its bird feet and races over to Na-nu to give the little demon a good licking.

"Who's a bad boy?" Na-nu asks it.

"I can't take any more of this," Spuck complains. "Just leave me here with the rest of the lost souls."

"Aw, come on," Adam says. "Compared to life in the universe, this is a piece of ration cake."

"I hope I live to taste a ration," Ham laments. "They sound delicious."

Face scrunched, the old space pirate says, "I wouldn't go that far. But there's other good stuff worth living for. Like, uh… well, I can't think of anything right now, but you know what I mean."

"No we don't!" Crom cries. "And we never will if we don't get out of here."

"Oh, right," he says, and grabbing one of his videotapes, he tells them, "So, let's go already."

Offering the fish head another sniff of his tape, Adam pretends to toss the memory down the next aisle, and the creature once again scurries off in fake pursuit. The kids slow their pace enough so the old space pirate can keep up as they nervously follow the demon child's pet monster down the labyrinth's darkest corridors. After running into more than a few dead ends, they start to argue about whether the goofy creature has any clue where it's taking them, when all of a sudden, they're there.

As the seven of them gaze out over a demon treasure trove the likes of which precious few souls have ever lived to bear witness, Adam prays, "*Am-stel.*"

## 91-123

When the grinning sun sets, The Park becomes a different world. All the booths are locked up and the aisles deserted, the great crowds of vacationing families having flown home for the modified dwarf planet's long night. But not everyone has left. As soon as the artificial lights replace the natural ones, another breed of fan emerges from the greasy shadows, come to the adult playground to engage in every type of illicit space activity known to nerd the only way they can still get away with it – in person. From collectible-laundering to back-booth trading card deals, it's true what they say about The Park after dark. The geeks come out at night.

I feel an indescribable sense of freedom staring up at the dark sky as I wander the shuttered aisles of Con City on my own for the first time. So, naturally, I head for the nearest beer cart.

But when I cross over to the other side of the aisle to avoid the wrath of an approaching dark magical girl and her entourage, I hear someone whisper to me from outside the entrance to the Jungle Gym, "*Psst*, over here."

Every space pirate worth their scrap knows to avoid the Gym at night, unless they want to be haunted by the ghosts of fads past. Taking the dark figure for a bootlegger, I tell him, "I don't do cards anymore. It's too painful."

"I got other stuff too. Come on, take a look." I jump back as a big furry alien waddles out of the shadows, but when he yanks off his bulbous costume head, it turns out he's just a Park kid. "You looking for Park pins?" he asks, opening a battered travel case covered in promotional stickers. "I got all the rare ones – even the discontinued 'sexy mascot' series."

"Nah, forget it," I tell him, even as I feel the collectible itch as I glance over his collection of Park exclusives. "I'm off that stuff."

"What about mind-altering substances?" he asks. "You look like a space head if I ever saw one."

"I resent that remark," I tell him. "But keep talking."

Carefully pulling at the bottom of his case, he opens a hidden compartment to reveal a wide assortment of forbidden candies and techno drugs. "Take your pick."

I try to make myself walk away, but as I finish perusing the explicit fantasy Pez dispensers, an unusual brick of sparkly translucent putty catches my eye. "What's that?"

"Oh, you wouldn't be interested in that," the kid says. "It's called hyperspace. But I think it might be a little advanced for you."

"Hey, if you're old enough to sell it, I'm old enough to smoke it," I tell him, impatiently motioning for his credit pad.

"*O-kay*," he says as he stuffs the sparkling brick into a cruddy customer space pipe. "It's your space funeral."

"I think it might be a little advanced for you."

I open my mouth to argue but suddenly decide better of it. "Maybe you're right. Gimme a brick of negative space and one of inner space."

"*O-kay*," the kid says, plucking out cubes of pure white and rainbow putty. "Just make sure you don't mix them."

"*Pfft*," I scoff. "I've been smoking since you were in space diapers. I think I know what I'm doing."

"*O-kay*," the kid says as he presents me with the brightest, reddest brick of putty I've ever laid eyes on. "But go easy. It might be a little stronger than whatever backspace chit you're used to smoking."

"*O-kay*," the kid says, a concerned look on his face as I wander off with a head full of space. "But I would advise against teasing the magical girls."

"*O-kay*...," the kid says, handing me a fresh red brick of space. "But I don't think you're supposed to eat it."

"And they sort of go on like that," Adam says. "All told, I figure I must have used up a couple dozen or so murrays wandering The Park over the next few space years."

"O-kay," Spuck says, lifting his battered sunglasses. "But shouldn't we be looking for your tape so we can get the fraiche out of here already?"

"Oh, right," the old space pirate says. "I guess I got distracted."

Securing his bag, Adam steps toward the center of the dark maze and the massive hoard of stolen memories stashed between its heaving walls. Mountains of death baubles fill every corner of the great chamber, spilling back out into the lifeless corridors of the labyrinth as if trying to escape. Except for the small patch of dead dirt where his class is huddled, the ground is completely obscured under piles of lost stuffed animals, holey concert tees, and abandoned virtual pets. He's sure his tape is somewhere amongst what he figures must be the biggest collection of universal paraphernalia in all of Other Side. The only problem is that it's offensively unorganized.

"So, where do we start?" Crom asks, tightening her green ponytail. "Enough with the kid stuff. I want to know what's on that tape."

"Kid stuff?" Adam grumbles.

"I mean, the last one was good-*ish*," she says. "But I have a feeling this one's going to be something special. It might even hold the secret to a good life."

Snorting, Spuck says, "I wouldn't get your hopes up."

"Come on, we can find it if we work together!" D'ohry chimes in, holding up the Pants sign.

"Or we can just let the fish head find it," Adam suggests.

He lets Na-nu's pet take a good long sniff inside his bag, and when he pulls the tapes away, the monster dives headfirst into the giant junk pile. The rest of them stumble after the creature as it navigates the nostalgic waters, but they soon lose track of it amongst the vast ocean of memories.

"It's swimming around like that superhero from your life," Ham says as he climbs over faded photographs and melted rubber wrestlers.

"Who, Namor?" Adam asks.

"No…"

"Stinky Diver?"

"*No,*" the kid says, with a degree of incredulity that makes his teacher feel both proud and annoyed. "That guy with all the money, what's his name? You know the one. He's kind of like you, doesn't like anyone near his stuff… *Scrooge McDuck*!"

"Oh yeah…," the old scrapper says. "That reminds me, be careful not to touch anything."

But it's too late. Choosing to ignore Adam's teachings, as usual, Spuck absently snatches one of the worn trinkets surrounding them and collapses onto the pile. His soul immediately begins sinking down into the junk, but before it gets swallowed up completely, Adam grabs onto the boy's arm and pulls him back out. When the memory attached to the Martian popping thing finally loosens its hold, Spuck lets go of the toy and gradually comes to.

"It's okay," Adam says, holding onto the kid. "You're back with us now, here in the labyrinth."

"*Aww,*" Spuck moans. "I was having the best memory. You weren't there, and you weren't there…"

"Yeah, well, sorry to wake you, sleeping dummy," Adam says. "But we're not out of this yet."

With their diminished powers combined, they resume their slog in pursuit of Adam's tape, when a strange piercing squawk suddenly echoes out across the memory pile.

"*Did we set off an alarm?*" Crom cries, her hands covering her ears.

But the alarm has a familiar ring to it, and when Adam notices Na-nu changing course toward the source of the noise, he yells, "*I think it's the fish head.*"

They find the yapping pet anxiously rolling around behind a stack of worn picture books as Na-nu tries to quiet its shrill cries. But it's no use.

"*Can't you get that thing to butt up?*" Spuck complains.

"*It's got my tape!*" Adam shouts, spotting the black rectangle stuck between the monster's fish lips.

But as he reaches out for his missing video, the memories shift under his feet, and he feels a sharp wave of pain in his side as his body is tossed into the ether. A moment later, he's crashing down onto a jagged pile of plastic action figures, and as the kids run to help him, his soul is pierced by a grating, bubbly howl more annoying than anything he's ever endured.

When Adam lifts his head, he sees the shadow of the beast stomping toward them, its massive hooves heedlessly crashing through the priceless collection. The monster towers over them, its body a cursed hybrid of angel and demon capable of tearing through the very fabric of Other Side. But it's the beast's ugly, misshapen head that shakes Adam's soul. Staring down at them through the face of a ruddy, sobbing infant with horns as black as space, the great demonoid releases a bowel-loosening cry.

"*This* is Asteroid Jones?" it booms. "The mighty space pirate?"

"So, you've heard of me," Adam says, clenching his holes as he stares into the beast's burning eyes.

"Your legend precedes you, even into the bowels of Other Side," the demon says. "But soon no one will ever hear of you again."

"Now wait just a space second!" Adam howls, briefly sending the demon back on its hooves. Turning to Nanu's pet monster, he yanks his tape out of the fish head's lips and gently lifts the precious memory into the ether. "Finally, after all that fishing around, my collection is almost complete, again."

**???**

I'm running late as I check over the report for the dozenth time, desperately searching for an error or miscalculation or whopping typo that will make this all miraculously disappear. But I know it's just wishful thinking. I was hoping to catch Mixr Buzplat alone before all the big heads showed up for the morning meeting, but I can already hear their witless banter on the other side of the door, completely unaware that their world is about to come crashing down. As soon as I step inside, I'm greeted by the obligatory hoots and hollers from the company's highest-ranking, most well-respected executives.

"I've been waiting to see that all morning," Mixr Nudnix remarks as I shuffle through the boardroom.

Normally I'd deliver a savage quip that would thoroughly emasculate him in front of all the other corporate chitheads, but I'm so frazzled from the information I'm about to deliver that all I can think to do is bonk him on his empty brain holder. This elicits a roar of laughter from the rest of them, and I can't help but think it will probably be their last. When I get to the head of the table, I hand the report to Mixr Buzplat, and he sets it aside before I can convey the urgency of its contents.

"Quiet down, quiet down," he tells the squawking gaggle. "Everybody shut your beaks. It's been a good year for Buzplat Food Services. Revenues are up, costs are down. Thanks to the latest advancements in flavor technology, we are now the largest manufacturer of foodstuffs on the planet. Of course, we owe the bulk of that success to our most popular snack, Soylent Pete."

"As if we weren't already exploiting their primitive backspace species enough," I mutter.

Each of the board members grabs a dehydrated meat stick from the baskets on the table and raises it in the air.

"Mixr Buzplat," I try to get his attention, but he's too busy chewing, so I snatch the report and hold it in front of his beady black eyes. "Mixr Buzplat, there's an important matter that requires your immediate attention."

"What is it, Mix Zorklar?" he finally asks, his face twisting as he bites into his snack stick. "And why aren't you eating?"

Angrily grabbing one of the sticks, I tear off a big chunk of meat and plead, "*I need you to look at this.*"

"All right, all right," he says, laughing as he flips through the pages. "Now what is this all about?" But as he reads over the report, the condescending smirk on his face fades, and his once infallible confidence quickly turns to quaking terror. "But this means…"

"That's right," I whisper, leaning in close so no one else can hear. "Soylent Pete *isn't* people!"

"But how could this have happened?" he whines.

"The clones must be smarter than we thought," I explain. "I told you it was a mistake to put them on the production line. Based on these reports, the original recipe was altered soon after the product launch."

"But then, what am I eating?" he chokes.

I shrug. "I don't think I want to know. We have to get out of here before—"

Just then, the door bursts open, and a rough-looking band of identical clones dressed in Buzplat coveralls marches into the boardroom.

Addressing the executives, their leader, a tall, hairy mammal of Earth origin says, "I trust I need no introduction."

My hands begin to sweat as Mixr Buzplat stands from his cushioned chair and whispers, "*Pete…*" His gray face covered in sweat, he suddenly grips the edge of the table and crashes to the floor.

"Just relax," the clone says as my heart flutters. "It'll all be over soon."

My legs wobble as the board members start falling out of their seats. Glancing down at the snack stick in my hand, my vision blurring, it's all I can do to mutter, "Oh fish…"

"And don't worry," Pete Prime says. "You won't go to waste."

"Ohhh, that's a good one," the baby-faced demon coos. "The suffering works on so many levels."

"Hey, this isn't mine!" Adam says, tossing the plastic memory back onto the pile. "It's not even labeled. Who does that?" He points his boney finger up at the blubbering beast and shouts, "Listen you, give me back my tape so I can go home and forget this whole stupid adventure ever happened."

Gazing down at the old space pirate the way a scrapper might regard a space roach, the great demon toddler's lips curl back, and it reaches its gnarled meat hook into its fanny pack. Teacher and class wait patiently as the beast roots around inside the giant neon satchel strapped around its waist, until it finally pulls out a familiar black rectangle.

Holding the tape up between its black claws, the demon says, "Is this what you're looking for? When I found out you had entered the labyrinth, I decided it would be wise to keep this memory close, though I never actually expected you to make it this far. In that sense, you did not disappoint."

"*My tape!*" Adam cries. "Give it here. It's mine. I want it."

A soft gurgle escapes the beast's crimson lips, and wrapping its beefy arms around its sides, it descends into a fit of unholy laughter. "You mean you've all sacrificed yourselves for one lousy death memory? Sure, it contains some decent suffering and adult situations, but it's not worth getting trapped in the labyrinth with me, King Dead, for the rest of eternity."

"That's what I've been trying to tell them," Spuck says.

"Well, I don't see what's so funny," Adam tells the demon. "It's my tape, and I want it back."

"It's just…" The giant baby pauses to stifle its howls. "I'm going to devour your souls. Not literally, but you get the idea. Well, maybe literally…"

Turning toward his students, huddled and whimpering in a heap of long lost memories, Adam instructs, "Run."

*"What?"* Crom whines, green tears dripping down her filthy face. "We can't leave you here. That thing is going to eat you up and spit you out. And by spit, I don't mean from its mouth."

"Don't worry," he says. "I got a plan. You guys wait for me in the maze while I get my tape back. If anything goes wrong, at least you'll still have a chance to find a way out. But I'll probably be fine. No demon can be as tough as this one looks. Now get out of here, while you still can."

Wrapping her arms around him like they do in the universe, Crom tells him, "Be careful, Mr. Jones."

"Let's go already," Spuck cries, having already retreated to the nearest tunnel.

Ham has turned catatonic, unable to take his eyes off the hideous beast, but D'ohry smacks him out of it and flashes Adam the Pants sign as she shoves the stupefied boy through the memory pile. Na-nu and his fish head pet are as indifferent as ever as they stumble after the others, and before the beast notices, the whole class is back inside the safety of the maze.

Seeing them battered and broken like that, and yet still willing to stick by him after everything, a fire sparks deep inside Adam's soul. What starts as just a flicker quickly grows into a raging inferno that manifests as a bright yellow aura flowing over the surface of his ethereal form.

The sight of him floating across the giant memory bin is enough to make the demon cease its cackling. "Oh ho. Your anger is showing, space pirate. Are you going to hurt me with your divine powers?" Waving the video over the scrapper's head, the demon says, "If you want this memory, you'll have to pry it from my immortal claws."

"I'll give you one chance," Adam tells the beast. "If you don't hand over the tape, I will have no choice but to bring the wrath of Rodney down upon you."

"You think you can defeat me?" The demon snickers, casting its fiery gaze upon the kids crowded in the tunnel behind the glowing spirit. "None of you will escape the wrath of *King Dead!*"

The old scrapper shakes his head and says, "When I unleash my incredible space pirate powers, you really will be king dead."

Despite all its big talk, when Adam approaches with his bright hand outstretched, the mighty beast falls into the throes of an all-out demonic tantrum. As the space pirate floats toward the thrashing creature, he suddenly feels himself rising up into the ether, and for a moment he believes he truly has gained control of his divine powers.

Then he looks down.

In the place where his stomach used to be, Adam finds a large demon horn as black as space, and he chokes out what he figures will end up becoming his famous last words, "Oh spit…"

# 124

"Can we go now?" Ferd complains into my helmet as we traverse the littered moonscape. "This place has been scrapped clean. The only thing we're going to find out here is space junk."

"Just a little further," Grandpa says. "There's something on the other side of that old Moon Burger billboard, or my name isn't Silas Ichabod Jones."

Trudging toward the grinning moon mascot, Ferd grumbles, "Pretty soon space pirates from around the universe will be doing all the scrapping for me. You'll see. *You'll all see!*" He turns his helmet to glance at me and clears his throat. "That sounded more menacing than I intended. But seriously, I can't wait to never scrap again. Are you sure I can't convince you to come work for me at the shop? The coffee's always hot and the donuts are rarely more than four space days old…"

"Thanks," I tell him. "But that'd mean I'd have to brush my hair, and get up early, and wear long pants. I'm a scrapper. I fly by the seat of my cargo shorts wherever the solar winds take me."

"Yep, this is it!" Grandpa announces. "I feel a big scrap coming on."

But when they round the side of the billboard, all they find is more junk.

Using his weighted boot to send a crumpled oil can sailing across the giant dumpyard, Ferd asks, "Can we go now?"

"My internal scrap detector must be on the fritz," the old man says. "I was sure we would find something good out here."

Much as it hurts to admit, I suggest, "Maybe Ferd is right. This place is a ghost moon. Why don't we head back to the ship, heat up some rations, and throw on a good splatstick."

"I'd rather get Moon Burger," Ferd says.

"After today's scrap, I don't think we can afford it," I inform him.

"Wait a space second," Grandpa says. "I think I see something."

"Aww, come on," I moan. "A scrapper can't survive on junk alone."

Waving me off, the old man lumbers toward a mountain of long-outmoded ship parts and begins rummaging through the pile. "Ahaha! I knew it. The old scrap sense is never wrong."

"What is it?" I ask. "Is it something good?"

Grandpa tosses away a few pieces of space trash and steps back to reveal an honest to Space God United Empires holo-display, in what appears to be very good to fine condition.

"Hold it," Ferd says. "I'll be the judge of what's good." He leans in close to give the device a closer inspection, and when he's satisfied, he announces, "Looks like it's Moon Burger for us!"

Grandpa eagerly gets to work hauling the machine out of the scrap pile, but even with the advantage of his old man strength, he can't get it to budge.

"Step aside, Grandpa," I tell him. "And make way for a new generation." But hard as I pull, shove, and curse, I can't move the thing either.

Shaking his helmet, Ferd grabs onto the other end, and when we all lift together, the display comes to life. For a moment, the artificial face looks out at us with curiosity and then the trash begins to quake under our boots. The junk pile shifts all around us as the old ship parts rearrange themselves, until they've formed a giant humanoid robot made of scrap. Grinning down from its expensive holo-screen as the three of us back up for dear life, the trash monster tells us, "In terms you can understand, you're about to be canceled."

"Anyway, it sort of reminded me of what's happening now," Adam sputters, staring down into King Dead's baby face as his spiritual body is gored by the beast's horn. "Not the TV spin-off, but the actual events that are occurring right at this moment."

"That didn't really happen," the demon argues.

"Yes it did."

"But the robot didn't really say that."

"Yes it did!" Adam insists. "I think."

"I've heard enough," King Dead booms, its eyes burning.

The old space pirate can feel his soul being ripped apart as the beast thrashes its miniature head. Somewhere down below, amongst the stolen memories, his students are crying out, helpless to reign in the demon's dark powers. His energy depleted, his body slips off its skewer and is flung across the vault. He crashes against something hard, and when he comes to, he's lying against the labyrinth wall, buried beneath a pile of memory objects.

As he struggles to move, the objects begin to fall away, until he's staring up at the dark sky surrounding Other Side. He can feel the tug of divine hands grabbing onto him, and suddenly he's being lifted up and laid to rest atop the great souvenir pile.

"Are you okay?" a being of divine light with a long green ponytail asks, and after a moment, he recognizes Crom and the rest of the kids staring down at him.

"I could use another cold one," Adam chokes. "But I seem to be alive. Maybe I didn't get hurt as bad as I thought." But when he lifts his head, he finds a large hole where his stomach should be.

"You stupid spitiot," Spuck says, scowling at the old space pirate through his cracked shades. "You risked your eternal soul just so you could show us another one of your deaths?"

"Aha," the old space pirate laughs, wincing at the pain shooting through his missing abdomen. "It wasn't just any death." He smiles and nods at the tape in his hand.

When the beast notices that Adam's memory has been snatched from its claws, it growls, "Well swiped, space pirate. But you won't live long enough to enjoy it. You and your friends are dead. Game over."

"We're not dead yet!" Adam tells the kids. "Quick, combine your mechas into a single ultra super holy robot powerful enough to destroy the demon."

"Uh," Ham's pixelated face flickers as he looks around at the rest of them. "That's not a thing."

"Rat farts," Adam says. "Once again I'm left to wonder what the fish BM has been teaching you over in that holy school. I guess it really is game over."

But as the demon stomps toward them, D'ohry cries, "Wait! Mr. Jones might be onto something. Maybe if we combine all of our holy powers, it will be enough to defeat the beast!"

"I doubt it," Spuck says.

"Butt up!" Crom cries. "D'ohry's right. We have to try."

"Fine," the boy relents. "I guess being obliterated is better than being stuck in here watching Mr. Jones's deaths for the rest of eternity."

"That's the spirit," the old space pirate croaks.

Standing between Adam and the ultimate evil, the kids' auras begin to glow as they channel their energy for one final attack.

"You think a few newborn spirits are powerful enough to defeat me?" the beast growls. "I am King Dead, dark lord of Other Side, eater of souls. Your powers are useless against—"

"Now!" Crom cries, and with their powers combined, the class unleashes a brilliant cascade of divine light bright enough to illuminate even the darkest corners of the unholy treasure room.

The beast dodges, but as if guided by the hand of Rodney, the blinding attack curves across the chamber and hits its target dead on. King Dead howls as it fights to overpower the bright beam, but it appears as though the demon has finally met its match.

"This is it," Crom cries. "Give it everything you've got!"

They hurl one final blast of holy energy at the beast, and it lands with a brilliant explosion that causes the dead ground to tremble beneath them.

As the kids collapse onto the junk pile, D'ohry says, "We did it!"

Adam manages to cough out a tired laugh, and soon they're all cracking up. The only one not joining in is Na-nu.

"I guess you feel kind of bad, helping us destroy your own kind," Adam says. "But don't worry. We don't want to hurt you. That demon was just a serious chithead."

Sighing, Na-nu shakes his head, and as he points across the chamber, his fish head pet lets out a terrified squawk. Adam turns toward the smoldering mass of memories in the center of the room, and his phantom stomach twists as a giant, petulant shadow rises out of the settling dust.

A soft whimper surfaces out of the destruction, the dying cries of a wounded demon. But as the sound echoes out over the great crypt, it gradually transforms into an earsplitting giggle. Emerging from the smoke with a twisted smile on its evil little face, King Dead looms over the fallen heroes and asks, "You didn't actually think that would work, did you?"

His voice weak and raspy, Spuck says, "Told... you."

"I might not eat that one," King Dead growls. "I like his style. Asteroid Jones on the other hand..." Lifting Adam by the leg, the demon grins and licks its lips. But as the beast stares at the old space pirate hanging helpless from its claws, a strange look comes over its face. If Adam didn't know better, he'd say it almost resembles pity. "On the other other hand, maybe we can make a deal." The demon sets the scrapper back down amongst his students and tells him, "If you hand over your tapes without a fight, I'll let the kids go."

"But you could just take them," Adam says. "Why trade at all?"

"Because a willing sacrifice carries with it a special kind of power," King Dead explains. "It will make your suffering all the sweeter. Anyway, my torture would be wasted on them. These kids haven't lived yet. They don't even know what pain is."

"Don't do it!" Crom pleads. "We won't leave you here to die by the claws of that big baby."

But looking at the broken spirits who gave their life energy to protect him, Adam slides his bag from around his neck and tells them, "Don't worry, I'll find a way out, somehow." He uses his last bit of strength to hurl his memory collection toward the demon, and for a moment at least, he is at peace. "Anyway, what's the worst that could happen? I'm already dead."

Eagerly slipping its claw through the bag's handle, King Dead lifts the treasure into the ether and bursts out laughing. "I can't believe you fell for that! You stupid space pirate. I'm never going to let any of you go. Your souls and your tapes are all mine!"

As the demon gleefully dances around the treasure pit, Adam tells the kids, "I guess I fished that up."

Wincing, Spuck laughs and tells him, "I think I speak for all of us when I say, no spit."

"Well, if this is the end, we might as well go out singing," D'ohry announces, her eyes twinkling.

"Don't you dare," Adam warns her.

But this time even his implied holy authority can't stop her from belting out the annoying lyrics, "Bum, bum, bum…"

# 125

Well, I guess this is it. With Ferd busy running his store and Grandpa too old to lift the heavy stuff, I'm on my own, just me and the *Asteroid Jones II*. Fuel and food are running low, and I'm down to my last beer. It's been space weeks since I scrapped anything good, and I'm starting to wonder how long I can keep this up.

My only company is the glowing box muttering paranoid taglines from the other side of the living room, *"What's in the basket?"*

I've been fortunate enough to have amassed a small video collection, but I've seen them so many times now that I know them by heart. When I finish re-watching the tape Brinx and I bought together all those space years ago, I don't even bother putting anything else on, opting instead to drift off to the soft sounds of analog snow.

Suddenly, I'm back at the old Misery Acres beverage store, searching through their clearance tapes. They must be trying to get rid of old stock because all the really expensive ones I've been eyeing are on sale for a few crits apiece. When I carry my haul up to the counter, the ancient alien who owns the place seems to have forgotten who I am, and he sells me two big bags full of rare videos without saying anything about the stolen ration.

But the moment I step outside, a screaming cyber girl runs up to me from out of nowhere and knocks the tapes out of my hands. As I check for damage, Jexxy yanks on my arm and pleads, "Wake up, space pirate!"

"Hold on," I tell her.

But before I can collect all the videos, she's hanging from my back and whispering in my ear, "*Wake up, wake up, wake up...*"

I feel my legs collapsing under her weight, and I open my eyes to find myself tumbling off the couch. For a long moment, I lay there with my face pressed against the cold living room floor, until I finally summon the strength to pick myself back up again.

Propped on the couch's edge, I snatch an old beer from the table and begin to choke down the dregs, when someone says, "*Finally.*"

By some miracle, I manage to hold onto the last of my precious suds as I jump up to search the dark cabin. But there's no one there.

"*Over here, space pirate,*" the digitized voice coos.

I don't want to look, but I can't help myself. When I turn my eyes toward the TV, Jexxy is staring out at me, her long silver hair pulled back over her electronic ear. "*Are you going to get over here, or what?*"

Shrugging, I crawl to the TV and press my lips to the screen. The speakers moan as our faces meld, and reaching through the glass, I fall into static.

"And I was never heard from again…," Adam says.

"What are you talking about?" Ham cries, flickering with exhaustion atop the memory pile as King Dead tries to decide which of the helpless souls to torture first. "Of course you were heard from again. I'm pretty sure that was just another movie."

"The worst part was that I somehow managed to break my VCR," the old space pirate laments. "It was space years before I scrapped another one."

"I think I'll tear the little demon apart first," the beast says, looking down on Na-nu and his fish head pet cowering in the back. "Or maybe I'll start with one of you young souls, to whet my appetite for the main course." Thick streams of saliva drip down the beast's chin as it turns its burning gaze on the old space pirate. "*Ooh*, am I going to enjoy torturing you…"

"*Ahem*," D'ohry squeaks, barely able to lift her rainbow head to admonish her teacher. "As I was singing, before I was so rudely interrupted, *bum, bum, bum*…"

Adam laughs bitterly, powerless to stop her. "Are you sure this is how you want to spend your last—"

But before he can say his piece, Crom, her voice wobbly with fear, cries out, "We're about to go on an incredible adventure, the opportunity for fun will be great!"

"What are you doing?" the demon demands.

"Life is an upside down illusion," Ham pants, bringing himself back into focus. "So grab it by the floppy ears and ride into the future!"

"Stop it!" the beast growls. "It's incredibly annoying."

"We're moving so fast through this universe that smells of tree nuts and sunshine," Spuck says. "Hang on tight to live your dreams!"

"*Arghhh*!" the childlike beast howls, covering its ears as it crashes to its furry knees. "As soon as you quit singing, I'm going to eat your souls."

As Adam watches the demon writhe amongst its collection of stolen memories, he experiences something he hasn't felt in a long time – hope. "I can't believe I'm singing this, but…" Summoning what little energy he has left, he shouts, *Go Pants Team Pink! Go Pants Team Pink! Fly into adventure!*"

"So you do know the words!" D'ohry cries.

"Of course I know the words," he says. "Now, it's time to *find the treasure at the end of time, and discover the love inside to teeter forward into a new day*!"

Its baby face twisted into an evil grimace, King Dead releases a desperate cry into the dark, "Rodney, protect me!"

The beast attempts a final feeble attack, but before it can get its claws on the old scrapper, he and his students sing, "*Go Pants Team Pink! Go Pants Team Pink!*"

When the words reach King Dead's pointy ears, the ancient demon grabs the sides of its diminutive head and wails as bright beams of light erupt from its holes.

All together, the class sings, "*Explode Pants Team Pink!*"

The beast lets out a final wounded howl, and its monstrous body bursts in a dazzling explosion of its own inner light.

As the light fades, the demon's dark blood and flesh rains down around the class like something from one of

Adam's horror tapes come to afterlife. For a while, he and the kids lie quietly amongst the carnage, too dazed to speak, much less move.

Once they regain enough of their strength, they huddle together to gaze out at the grisly aftermath, unsure whether to laugh or cry at the gory scene. So, they do both.

"Shouldn't somebody say something?" D'ohry asks.

"Sure," Adam says. "Good riddance and *am-stel*." But just as he finally, mercifully begins to let his guard down, the ground begins to shake. "What? What'd I say?"

"Oh great," Spuck complains. "You just had to say something!"

"She told me to!" Losing his balance as the tremors intensify, the old scrapper tumbles down the shifting memory pile and crashes to the bottom with the rest of his class. Pulling his head out of the fish head's mouth, he cries, "What is it now, some sort of super ultra mega demon? We'll beat that too! We can take anything this stupid place can conjure up. We'll fight off demons for the rest of eternity if we have to."

"Speak for yourself," Spuck says.

As the living dead walls of the labyrinth tremble and glow all around them, Crom screams, "*What's happening now*?! Not the show."

Gathering his last scrap of energy, Adam prepares his old soul to stand in defiance of whatever Other Side plans to throw at them next, when the walls begin to crumble. But instead of collapsing in on the space pirate and his students, the souls that sacrificed themselves to hold the demon at bay begin to leave their posts and float off into the ether.

"That's what I thought," Adam says as the labyrinth gradually dissolves around them. "Now, finally, let's get the fish out of here."

Climbing over the rubble, Ham asks, "What about all this stuff? Are we just going to leave it here?"

"It'll be fine," the old scrapper says as he stumbles through the giant memory dump. "Now that it's outside the confines of the labyrinth, it'll all eventually fade and return to its original owners."

"Hold up," Spuck says, straightening his cracked shades. "You mean, we could have just *waited* for your memories to come back and skipped this whole nightmare?"

"Well, yeah," Adam tells the kid. "But that could take an eternity. I want to watch them now." Searching through the beast's remnants, he retrieves his bag of tapes, stained black with demon blood, and methodically counts them. "Good, they're all here. Now, for the love of Rodney, *let's go.*"

But as the class plods back toward the ghost wood, a horrifying wail emerges from the memory pile. With more than a little reluctance, they follow the muffled cries to a squirming heap of exploded demon guts. The kids unanimously vote that Adam should be the one to dig through the unholy remains, and tossing aside big hunks of charred monster flesh, he uncovers a sobbing demon baby with burning eyes and horns as black as space.

# PART III

# (Re)Birth

126.-

Adam rocks the goopy demon baby in his arms as a sliver of divine light materializes at the edge of the dark forest. Thanks to the news of King Dead's demise and the destruction of the labyrinth, the last leg of their journey has gone a lot smoother. Their legend has spread so fast that they haven't been hassled by a single demon the whole way.

"Well, I've only got a couple deaths left," Adam tells his class as they approach the end of their lesson.

"Spare us," Spuck says, his sunglasses so bent out of shape that they'll barely stay on his head. "We already learned about those deaths. It was part of that whole black gold saga."

"Oh yeah…" For a brief moment Adam's mind drifts off into another world. "I almost forgot about the black gold. Maybe when we get to Daizy's we'll watch the last one anyway."

"What for?" the boy asks. "All of Other Side knows about that one."

Sighing, the old space pirate says, "If you don't know the answer to that by now, then Rodney help you."

As they come to the end of the ghost wood, the kids' auras begin to regain some of their luster, and he can sense their spirits lifting.

"We made it!" Crom cries. "*We actually made it.*"

"With Asteroid Jones as your teacher, did you ever have any doubt?" Adam asks.

"Uh…" She pauses to think about it. "No."

Just when it seems as if nothing else could possibly prevent them from escaping their shared nightmare, a ghostly voice whispers, "You're not going to make it."

"Aww, fish off, would you?" Adam whines as the annoying ghost materializes in front of them. "We *are* going to make it. The woods end right there, see? It's over."

The lost soul stops dead in the path, when a dark shadow suddenly pounces out of the ghost wood and wrestles it to the ground.

As they roll around in the dead dirt, Adam catches a glimpse of the cat's furry tail and demands, "Where have *you* been? We could have used your help. While you were fooling around, our souls almost got devoured."

"From what the demons have been screaming as I feasted on their flesh, you did more than fine without me," Ol' Garth purrs, jumping off the ghost to rub up on Adam's legs, its fur matted with demon blood. "And you look really… good."

"You *are* going to make it?" the ghost moans to itself, repeating the words over and over as it dazedly wobbles off into the shadows. "You *are* going to make it. You *are* going to make it…"

Watching the annoying spirit finally fish off back into the forest, Adam suddenly bursts into tears. "I really hated that ghost."

The kids point and laugh at him, but when they finally step out of the dark woods and into the bright pasture beyond, there's not a dry eye in the class. Even Na-nu and his fish head pet start blubbering.

For a long while they lay in the long grass recounting the worst moments from their adventure, until an old soul happens by who can direct them to Daizy's place.

"Sure, everybody around here knows Daizy," the wrinkly wanderer says, straightening his beard as he points far off into the distance. "It's just over that hill there. It's a bit of a walk."

"I think we can handle it," Adam says. "Thanks."

"Happy to be of service." Before they wander too far, he adds, "But a word of warning – be careful playing around these woods. I don't want to scare the kids with any horror stories. But it's dangerous in there."

Shooting his students a knowing glance, Adam tells the old codger, "We'll try to remember that."

As they cross the bright pasture, their wounds begin to heal and their soiled, ripped clothes gradually repair themselves. By the time they reach Daizy's moon shack, they show almost no signs of ever having been inside the dark forest. The only thing that hasn't reverted back to the way it was before they left is Spuck's sunglasses.

"*What?*" the boy asks as the rest of them stare at his broken frames. "I think they look krule."

"This place is so cute!" D'ohry cries, admiring the bright garden surrounding the little round domicile.

"Wait here," Adam tells them, before heading up the worn path leading to the house, the devil baby cooing in his arms. Taking a deep breath, he knocks and calls, "Daizy?"

No one answers, but the door is cracked, so he gently pushes it back and steps inside. The room is still, bright sunshine and warm breeze spilling in through the open windows. She's not home, but he can feel her in every manifested molecule of the place. The big kitchen-slash-living room is scattered with old photos, *Super Sentai* action figures, and other memory objects, many of which he recognizes from times when the two of them were together. Somehow he didn't realize she cared about this stuff. She was never much of a collector.

When he's finished looking at the unfinished space witch costume hanging on the wall, he moves to the cluttered table in the center of the room, where he spots a familiar plastic rectangle. Eagerly snatching the tape, he bemoans the poor condition of the label, when he notices there's a note scrawled across it – "*See you space pirate…*"

Someone suddenly enters the doorway, radiating a brilliant light, and Adam calls, "Daizy?" But as the light form steps inside the shack, he quickly recognizes the red hair and holier-than-thou grin of his guardian angel. "Oh, it's you…"

"Don't act so happy to see me," Buttmuncher says.

"I've got nothing to say to you," Adam tells the angel, stomping across the room and back out into the bright yard.

"What's your problem?" the light form complains as it chases after the hobbling space pirate.

"What's *my* problem?" Adam cries, waving his tape in the ether. "You sent us into that stupid maze to get kidnapped, skewered, eaten, and worst of all, robbed of my precious video memories. It's a miracle we made it out with all my tapes intact." Stopping in his tracks, he spins around and shoves the demon baby into BM's arms. "Here, you take care of whatever this is."

"Hey, where's Daizy?" D'ohry asks. "I want to meet her."

"She's not here," Adam says, glancing at the angel. "Is she?"

"No," BM says. "She went back. But you can see her again."

Plopping down in the grass next to Ol' Garth, Adam adds the tape from the house to the rest of his collection and sulks. "So, that's what this was all about, some divinely convoluted way to get me to go back to life?"

"Well, yes." The angel gazes on Adam with genuine compassion, but it just annoys the old space pirate even more. "But that's not the only reason. It was also to get these young souls ready to live their own lives. From what I witnessed, I chose the perfect scrapper for the job. Plus, I bet they taught you a thing or twenty."

"Yeah, I learned to keep a closer eye on my stuff," he complains, and whipping his head up, "Wait a space second. You mean you were following us? *You could have helped?*"

"Sure," BM says. "But what fun would that be? Anyway, we better get moving. You can leave your tapes. You won't need them where you're going. Don't worry, you can watch them when you get back."

With a sigh of resignation, Adam opens the bag to look over his deaths one last time and says, "But they won't be the same, will they?"

The angel smiles but doesn't argue.

"You're taking him already?" Cromula cries. "Aren't we going to watch the last tape at least?"

Laughing, Adam reluctantly gets back on his feet and hands her the bag. "She erased it…"

"Since that's settled," BM says, motioning for them to gather around. "I think that's enough learning for one adventure. Everyone, hold on."

The whole class, plus Na-nu and his pet, puts their dirty paws on BM's pristine t-shirt, and as soon as Adam presses his finger to the angel's face, they're all instantaneously transported to a great white void containing nothing but an oversized space bubble.

"Whoa, that's the universe?" Ham asks, his spirit back to full resolution as he stares up at the dark sphere. "It's so… big."

For a short while, the class quietly gazes into the miraculous bubble, until BM finally tells them, "Okay, everybody say your goodbyes."

"Well, I guess this is—" Adam starts to lecture, when the kids suddenly tackle the old space pirate, sobbing as they crush him in a holy hug.

"We'll never forget what you taught us, Mr. Jones," Crom wails, her green tears staining his t-shirt. "I took really good notes."

D'ohry, sparkling as bright as ever, tells him, "You're the best teacher I ever had." Glancing back at BM she adds, "No offense."

"*Ha!*" Adam taunts the angel.

"This is sadder than that movie from your life," Ham moans.

"I never did get to finish watching *The Stupids*, again," the scrapper complains.

Even Spuck sheds a tear behind his broken sunglasses. "I guess you weren't so bad. I mean, we survived, somehow."

"I'm going to miss you," Na-nu says, and they all turn to look at the lesser demon, their mouths hanging open. "Hey, I told the truth! *I did it again!*"

Finally shoving them away, Adam says, "I have one more lesson for you, and this one applies the same in Other Side as it does in the universe – you have to know when to let go."

Placing a hand on Adam's shoulder, BM tells the old space pirate, "It's time."

"What if I decided I didn't want to go?" Adam asks. "My old soul is so tired. I don't know if it'll survive the trip."

"Come on, you don't really want to stay here," the angel says. "You were stagnating, locked up in that shack with your death tapes. Anyway, you're only as old as you think you are."

Adam glances down at his aching hands and says, "No, I'm pretty sure I'm just old."

"Close your eyes." His guardian angel is just so dam kind and patient, Adam decides to humor the ackle. "Now imagine a time when you were young, one in which the fog of memory and prophecy was nonexistent and your place in the grand scheme of things irrelevant. Notice the sensation of being, unencumbered by a lifetime of pain and regret. Remember how it feels to be alive in an infinite and ever-expanding universe in which all things are possible. Now open your eyes."

Adam impatiently does as he's instructed, and he looks back down at his hands to find that they're a little less wrinkly and a lot stronger than he remembered. He manifests a mirror, and the same old space pirate is reflected back at him, only half a lifetime younger than when he last looked.

"Told you," BM says. "Now, will you come on? You're not the only soul I have to look after."

"Wait, who's going to watch after Ol' Garth and the rest of my pets?" Adam asks. "And what's going to happen to the demon baby?"

Shoving him toward the bubble, BM says, "The baby will be fine. I'll raise it as competently as I would any other soul. As for your pets, I thought I would look after them, while utilizing your house as a learning aid for teaching new souls about the harsh reality of life in the universe. Before you complain, the place won't fade as fast with someone living in it. If you hurry, it might even still be here when you get back."

"Fine, but don't let anybody touch my—" Adam starts to instruct but thinks better of it. "Eh, let 'em touch whatever they want." Looking up at the big space bubble, he muses, "Life in the universe… It seems like so long ago. How long has it been, anyway? A thousand space years?"

"That's a fundamentally meaningless question, but if I remember the conversion right…" The angel's teenage face twists as it calculates. "I guess it's been something like… two."

"Millennia?"

"Months."

"*That's all?*" Adam yelps. "Fish, it feels like an eternity. Maybe it's good that I'm going back. Except, I was thinking about visiting my parents first, and what about Grandpa? Whatever happened to him?"

"I have a feeling you'll run into them sooner than you think," BM says. "Now, get out of here, will you?"

"All right, all right, let me just say one last goodbye to *my* students." Waving to his class, Adam calls, "Good luck on the other side. Don't do anything I would do. And remember what Rodney say – *relax.*" Turning to gaze into the majesty of the universal bubble, he takes a deep breath of ether and prepares to take the plunge. But as he glances back for one last look at his friends, something else catches his eye, little more than a dark smudge in the distance. "Hey, what's that?"

"Oh, that's nothing," BM says. "It's just one of the other universes."

"*Other universes?*" Adam cries. "You mean this isn't the only one?"

"Of course not," the angel grumbles. "Look around you. There are infinite universes."

"Whoa…" Peering out across the void, the old space pirate suddenly notices little smudges all over the place, marring the otherwise perfect emptiness. "So, are they all just slight variations of this one? Like, there's a version of me in one of the other universes with an even more impressive video collection?"

"*What?*" the angel howls, its near-infinite patience having finally run out. "*No.* I mean, maybe. They're all different, each more magnificent and inconceivable and awe-inspiring and so on than the last. Actually, this one is closer to what you might call a 'beginner' universe."

"Beginner?" Adam croaks. "So, is this place, like, the topmost level of reality?"

"Yes, of course," BM says.

"How do you know?"

"Uh…" The angel thinks for a moment and finally says, "Never mind how. I just know."

"Hey, that reminds me," Adam says. "Whatever happened to my Chibi Sitcom cards? I lost track of them at some point and always wondered where they went."

"Jexxy pawned them for two bricks of hyperspace."

"*I knew it!*"

"Now please, I'm begging you," the angel says. "Get the fraiche out of here."

Adam raises his index finger as he thinks of a few hundred more questions to ask, but when he sees the light blazing in Buttmuncher's eyes, he decides to save them for next time. Turning toward the dark bubble, he sighs deeply, and with a tired laugh, he dives back in.

The first thing I notice when I enter the universe is how fishing cold it is. I want to tell someone to turn up the heat as I'm ripped screaming from the comfort of my dark dwelling and thrust into the lurid light of reality, but I never get the chance.

"Whoops," The sterile monster carrying me mutters as it fumbles me in its clumsy hands. "Almost lost you."

I'm swiftly transferred into the arms of a sedated, yet infinitely more careful being, and for some reason beyond my understanding, I suddenly calm down.

Tearing its attention away from the glowing box in the corner of the room, the strange being gazes down at me while a bigger, dumber creature points at the box and laughs, "Ha, Car hole… Somehow that one never really sunk in bef——" When it sees me, it turns away from the screen and pokes my arm, as if to confirm I'm real. "What're we gonna call him?"

"I was thinking of naming him after that guy, with the sled," the one holding me says, its thin hair matted with sweat.

"Who, Orson Welles?"

"No, the other one – Silas Marner."

"There was no sled in Silas Marner. You must be thinking of Ethan Frome."

"Sled or no sled," the sweaty one says, "that's the name I was thinking of. And for his middle name, what about that ghost with the horse and the pumpkin head – Ichabod Crane."

"That's not the name of the horseman. It's the guy the horseman was chasing."

"Whatever…" The sweaty creature smiles down at me, and as I begin to doze in her arms, she says, "It's a pleasure to meet you, Silas Ichabod Jones. Welcome to the universe."

# Author's Note

This was probably not the book you were expecting. It's not the book I originally intended to write. But as I was working my way through *More Space Junk*, the pieces just started falling into place. I knew I wanted to revisit the afterlife while also delving deeper into Adam's past and future.

For me personally, this book served as an exploration into some of my own feelings about the beginning, the end, and everything in between. So, what did I learn? What is the true purpose of life, the universe, and everything? Fish if I know.

# About the Author

Andrew Bixler emerged from the same nightmare as Wes Craven. He writes fiction that'll blow your mind right out of your brain holder. He is also co-host of Big Orange Couch: The 90s Nickelodeon Podcast.

For more about the author, news about upcoming books, and contact information, visit **andrewbixler.com**

For more about the Big Orange Couch podcast, visit **bigorangecouch.podbean.com**

# Thanks for Reading

I am grateful that you chose to spend your hard-earned crits on my book. If you enjoyed this book, please spread the word to every sci-fi adventure fan you know. The fate of my world depends on it!

# How Was the Ride?

If you've come this far, maybe you're willing to come a little further. I am an independent author, and I can use all the feedback I can get. Let me know what you think of this book by leaving a review on Amazon, Goodreads, or by shooting me a message!